A Sometimes Strange Story

a novella

Uri Norwich

Published by "highwood publishing new york©"

For information regarding permission, contact
highwoodpublishingny@gmail.com

ISBN-13: 978-1541118669
ISBN-10: 1541118669

Cover and Back Cover Design by URI NORWICH

Manufactured in the United States of America

Also By Uri Norwich

"Russian Jews Don't Cry"© 2013-2016

"The American Deluge"© 2014

"If I Was Real..." ©2013-2016

DEDICATION

to Jason, a son, if I had another one

CONTENTS

Disclaimer

This book is a work of fiction. Names, characters, events, and incidents are the products of the author's imagination or are used fictitiously. Any resemblance to real individuals, living or dead, events, and places is entirely coincidental. Still, some names of my family members are preserved as they were.

1. A Job Offer

My boss called me in. When I walked into his office, he got up, walked around his desk, and sat on the very edge of it with one foot on the floor.

"What would you say if I offered you a job in Italy?"

He stared at me as if he just presented me with a big bonus check for a job I had never done. His loose foot kept swinging like a pendulum, mesmerizing me and not letting concentrate on his words. I was glued to it, thinking, *"Could he afford a better pair of shoes? For crying out loud, he probably makes three times more than I do… And those hideous socks?"* Now my attention switched to his black, brown and beige argyle-patterned high socks. *"Let me tell you, my friend, no Italian man could be caught dead wearing anything like that."* I thought.

"So?" He was waiting for my response.

His voice took my attention off his *"argyles." "Yes, of course, he wants to know if I would take a job in Italy…"* My thoughts raced through my head with a speed of a movie fast-forwarded on the screen, except running the other way, five years back.

*****

My hands were trembling when I handed a large manila envelope to an Immigration officer at the Terminal 1 of the JFK International airport. He shook its content out on the counter, carefully looked inside, making sure that nothing was left, and quickly grabbed one paper. It was the second most important document in my life. The first most important document I held in my hands was four years ago. It was a letter of acceptance to College of Electrical Engineering of the Polytechnical University. In the Soviet Union, all men accepted into college were exempt from mandatory army draft. That reason alone was the greatest motivator for kids to get into a higher education institution. It was certainly for me.

The officer examined my entrance visa, carefully studying every seal and signature on it. Then he got up and walked away from the counter still holding my visa in his hands. My heart sunk down in my shoe, and remained there until he showed up holding a big black ledger in his hands. I noticed that a piece of paper was sticking out between the pages. I couldn't breathe.

"Congratulations, young man!" he said matter-of-factly. I still couldn't breathe.

"Welcome to the United States of America!"

I stood there numb as if a bucket of ice water was dumped on me. He noticed my condition and cheerfully continued,

"Here are all your papers, back in the envelope. In a day or two, get yourself to the Social Security office, they will set you up so you can look for a job. Is anyone meeting you?" He looked at me smiling. I nodded.

"Well, welcome again to the greatest country in the world! Good luck! You will need it."

A few months later, I found myself in West Hartford, Connecticut. A chain of lucky events led me to end up there. After four weeks in New York City, I realized that it wasn't my kind of living. Although back in the Soviet Union, I grew up in a large city with over a million inhabitants, I had always had an easy access to wild nature. Of course, New York City need not be compared to anything in the world. One could always argue that I would've found anything there if I only wanted to. In the end, the hustle and bustle of the large metropolis drove me nuts. I started looking for a place to move out, but where to? It was not an easy task.

America is a large country. Although it stretches for twenty-five hundred miles from coast to coast, it is not as large as the Soviet Union once was, with its ten time zones and sixty-two hundred miles of land. I had sent my resume to every major utility in the United States, offering my engineering expertise. Slowly but surely, I had been collecting a pile of *"thank you for your inquiry, but at the current time…, and blah-blah-blah"* polite letters. When the last response arrived, I finally realized that perhaps the Soviet engineering degree was not good enough for this country. There was not anyone to advise or help me with anything, until some lucky day.

I had spent the Labor Day holiday on the only beach I could get to by subway. It was the Brighton Beach. Looking at my former compatriots putting their roots there, made me want even more to get away from New York. At the time, most of the people who had chosen to settle down there had arrived from former Soviet Republics of Ukraine and Moldavia. Generally, people from Russia, and especially who had lived in large cities, had nothing in common with those folks. For the Americans, a large influx of the Soviet immigrants was a novelty. For the first time since the WWI, large groups of white people had been arriving from Europe. The Americans almost forgot that there was an immigration of the white people, who had founded this country in the first place. The majority of the new arrivals were Jewish. The Jewish communities around the country opened their midst to the Soviet immigrants. That was a benefit. The government did their huge part, helping resettle thousands of uprooted and displaced people.

That Labor Day, I had joined a small group of folks on the beach who had been already in America for a while. When I was asked what I was doing for the coming Jewish holiday of Rosh Hashana, I shrugged my shoulders. What could I say?

I didn't know anyone yet in the entire country. Somehow, I got invited to attend the celebrations at the Jewish Center of West Hartford.

Growing up in the Soviet Union, the only religion I was exposed to was atheism. Atheism was taught as the only and absolute truth. It was taught *"from diapers to coffin"* — the Russian way of saying *"from womb to tomb."* Colleges and universities taught mandatory atheism course where dedicated professors declared that science had proven that there was absolutely no God, period! Oddly enough, those professors were always old, dressed in the most worn-out suits, some had gray beards with remains of the last meal, and spat saliva out of their mouth. At the time, the latest proof of "no existence of God" was the Russian cosmonaut *Yuri Gagarin*, who had been the first man flown in the outer space and around the Earth. Many others had followed him and had not seen any gods out there, yet.

And then, there was Darwin, of course. Charles Darwin must've been sent by communist god, or the devil, to test people on the planet Earth. The Soviets embraced his crazy theories as absolute scientific proof that God had been invented by the sick capitalist imagination to force people to work for nothing. Every time my parents took me to the Zoo, I tried to spend most of the time by the gorilla cage, ignoring other animals and aggravating my family. I was hoping to catch that miraculous moment of the transformation of the ape into a man, our teachers kept insisting had happened. I didn't entirely ignore other animals. Snakes too kept me glued to their large, brightly lit glass cages in a pitch-dark room. I kept watching them, afraid to miss a precious moment when they would start growing legs and turn into alligators, or dinosaurs. I suppose, they were the next animals on the Darwin scale of so-called evolution.

Practicing religion was banned and prosecuted in the Soviet Union. From the early days after the 1917 October Revolution, religion had been pronounced *"The opium poisonous to the people."* It had been forced underground into exile. Churches had been destroyed, either burned or turned into potato warehouses. Temples and mosques had been demolished. On Stalin's orders, the Cathedral of Christ the Savior, built in 1812 to commemorate the defeat of Napoleon, had been erased to make way for the open-air public swimming pool. Religious traditions had been preserved in the families, and never publicly discussed for fear of prosecution.

My family never practiced any religion. My parents worked hard to hide our ethnicity, trying to blend into the Soviet society. There was nothing Jewish in our home. Yet, even as a boy, I had always been aware of our heritage. For starters, the Internal Passports of my parents clearly stated "Jew" in the infamous paragraph number five.

My family kept a big secret for many years. Later on, I found out that many Jewish families had skeletons in their closets too. No one dared to bring them to life, fearing prosecution. Since I was a child, I remembered overhearing whispers between my grandparents and my mother about a mysterious woman who lived in a faraway land called Israel. She was never discussed in spite of my occasional attempts to find out more. Every time I tried asking about her, I was put immediately in my place. Until one day…

I knew that something was going on. Every night, my Grandfather Pinkus was glued to a radio, trying to catch bits and pieces of any Western radio broadcast breaking through heavy jamming. The radio stood on a small table by the window in the living room of our apartment. That living room served also as my bedroom at night. I lay on my folding sofa-bed pretending to be asleep. Grandpa would stay till very late at night, refusing to go to bed, until he could get at least some information. Of course, the next morning, the Russian propaganda machine reported that their Arab friends had been advancing in their war for freedom from the Israeli oppressors. Grandpa's nightly vigil lasted for a week. On June 10, 1967, in the Six Day War, Israel had defeated millions of crazy Arabs wishing its demise.

That morning, I saw my Grandma Dora's face lighting up and shining as I had never seen it before. On that day, she told me the big secret. She had a younger sister Sonia. Fifty years ago when my Grandma's family lived in the Black Sea port-city of Odessa, they had to escape and hide in the countryside. It was too dangerous to remain in the city. The Western armies were fighting the Red Army, trying to recapture Odessa from the revolutionary Bolsheviks. There was that proverbial last boat to Turkey, departing from the torn by the Civil War Russia. Sonia was young and single. She was seeing ("dating" wasn't invented yet, just like the global warming) a young fellow who talked her into sneaking their way onto that boat. Dora was single too, but she was also the older sister of three siblings and decided to stay with her parents to help in the countryside. By that time, Dora had graduated the Teachers Academy and earned her degree in teaching math. Finally, that explained that half a century later I would telephone her for help every time I got stuck with my math homework.

Just before Sonia got on the ship, Dora handed her the Teacher diploma. Grandma Dora knew that her little sister would get a better use out of it than herself staying behind in Russia. Hugging Sonia, she was sure that it was the last time she would ever see her again. With these last words, Sonia was gone forever. She had been gone for the next fifty years, blocked from the rest of her family by the Iron Curtain, by wars and by the craziness of the world. Until that very day! On that day, Grandma Dora told me about Sonia. I was listening, afraid to breathe and in fear that the story could interrupt at any moment, and I would never learn what happened next.

And what happened next was, Grandma Dora decided to contact her sister Sonia in Israel. She decided the time had come to announce to the world that she was not afraid anymore. She started writing letters to Sonia every week, hoping that one of them could find its way through the censorship cracks. One of the letters did.

We received a reply from Sonia. She was alive and well in Israel. It just happened that the very first Sonia's letter arrived in September of 1967. Inside the envelope, we found a breathtakingly beautiful card with the Jewish New Year- Rosh Hashana wishes. We had never seen anything like that before.

The arrival of a new year in the Soviet Union had been always celebrated, oh well, on New Year's Day. It had no religious meaning — just a pretty winter holiday with the New-Year-tree and gifts found under it. My grandparents and even my father still remembered from their childhood the meaning of Jewish Holidays. So that card was a perfect occasion to start my religious education. That was how I got my first explanation about God, the seven days of Genesis, and other pretty stories from the Bible. There were no temples; there were no rabbis or priests; there was no religion in the Soviet Union, period!

The Jewish Temple in West Hartford, I was taken to for the celebrations, was called Congregation Beth Israel or House of Israel. The ceremony itself was quite boring. Everyone was holding a book. That was "The Book," as I was told. The Rabbi behind the pulpit on stage was reading and the crowd periodically was responding to him. A man with a good voice kept singing some verses from the same Book, accompanied by a piano player. I tried, but couldn't make out a word, except for *"amen."* I asked if they had a book in Russian. They didn't. Everything was in Hebrew with some English translation. Out of boredom, I started watching people, trying to guess how many of them had no idea what the rabbi was reading. I could tell that there were enough characters who were barely trying to make till the end of the service. And yet, the majority looked involved and participating. A young woman was playing the piano. She wore high basketball *"keds,"* looking totally out of place. I suppose they helped her with pushing on the pedals below. Later on, I was explained that Orthodox Jews were not allowed to wear leather shoes during the Hi-holidays to demonstrate suffering from daily comforts and concentrate on regrets for past misdeeds. Well, it wasn't an Orthodox temple, and *"keds"* were as comfortable as any leather shoes could be. Besides, they were in high fashion at the time.

Regardless of my thoughts, I enjoyed the service. The arrival of the Jewish New Year gave me the very first opportunity to witness the open celebration of religious spirit. It wasn't a quiet underground prayer of oppressed people, but humble and yet beautiful expression of freedom. That was an entirely new experience. Yet, I had taken it as it was a natural and long-deprived habit I forgot about. I felt that I had always been aware of its presence, but never saw it come to life. I felt that I somehow belonged there. For the first time, I felt that I got to the right place. The place, I could call home…

It seemed that everyone was relieved when the service finally ended. People were kissing each other and wishing a Happy

New Year. It sounded so strange that so many folks wished me a Happy and Healthy in the middle of September. I had to get used to it yet. When just a few people remained in the synagogue, the rabbi came over to me and asked if I was a guest of someone. He had never seen me before. I tried explaining with my limited English but luckily was helped by my friends. They themselves were guests of someone in the congregation. Then it happened so fast, we all ended up sitting around a large table in the hall in the back of the temple. In another hour, I had my first job interview set up for the next week.

I didn't have a car, nor did I have any means to afford it. The night before, I looked up on the map where I had to go. It was a long trip. I started early, taking a 6 a.m. Metro-North out of the Grand Central Station. In Hartford, I had to change to another train taking me further east to a small town of Manchester. When I finally emerged from the train after almost four-hour ride, I found myself in the middle of nowhere. A bright fall sunshine spilled its golden rays over endless green rolling hills. *"That is my kind of living,"* I caught myself thinking. I deeply breathed in the light breeze blowing from nearby fields full of freshly dried hay. Then I fished out a business card from my slack's pocket and dialed a number.

When I asked for the person whose name was printed on the card, at first, I thought that they hung up on me. I still could hear breathing on the other end. The lady asked if I wanted to talk to the person, making sure I wasn't mistaken. I read the last name from the card. She switched me to another lady who told me not to move from where I was standing and hung up. I didn't know if I understood her, but I didn't move an inch from the telephone on the station wall. I started feeling pressure growing inside but kept standing… I didn't know how much longer I could hold. A few minutes went by, I couldn't hold it any longer. I limped my way to the station entrance. I couldn't walk straight, such a load I was carrying inside. A man in shabby clothes was standing by the door. His entire look was unkempt and disheveled. I asked him to watch for someone looking for me, hoping that he understood my broken English. He grinned and said something. I could smell his bad breath and a strong odor emitted by his persona.

The first thing I saw emerging from the station was a large, white Cadillac. Two men were standing in front of it. One of them was my bum. He was vividly articulating with his hands, constantly pointing with one of them towards the building. The only word I could catch was a "bathroom." He finally noticed me and stepped aside making a curtsy and pointing at me. The other man turned around. He was a medium height, well-dressed in light–gray suit and good-quality leather shoes. The shirt was unbuttoned at the top exposing a small golden letter H. His face was thin with dark eyes and a light-color hair brushed to one side. The man was cleanly shaved. He stared for a moment as if trying to remember and then made two big steps towards me with stretched out hand. His shake was firm and confident.

"Hi, I am Joseph Wieber. Remember me from the temple last week…"

As if I could forget my first-ever job interview in America. Meanwhile, he continued,

"Glad you could make it. Please, get in the car."

He opened the front door for me. As he started going around the car to his side, he suddenly stopped, dipped his hand into the pocket of his pants and fished out a bill. He handed it to the man who watched out for me. Then he got inside,

"Do you speak Yiddish?"

I didn't. In the old times, Yiddish was the language of the European Jews in everyday life. I remembered that my Grandfather Pinkus and Grandma Dora, if they wanted to hide something from me, would conspire in Yiddish. The funny thing was that with time, I learned some words and picked up even some expressions. I never revealed my understanding of their conversations and always played along.

"Too bad," he continued. "You know, I too came to this country from Europe. They were different circumstances and different times. My mother and I had to escape Austria after the Nazis took it over in 1938. We were lucky to immigrate to America. My dad didn't survive." He sighed deeply.

We were driving between harvested fields. The trees started turning into the colors of autumn. The wind was playing with Joseph's hair, making him constantly brush them off his face with one hand. He kept the other one firmly on the wheel. I had never been in such large American car. And to top it all, it was a Cadillac…

"You see these fields," he pointed out. "I worked those every day after school. During the war, they used to grow tobacco here. Every able teenager at my school helped. We had to win the war. From the very first day we came off the Ellis Island onto this blessed land, I was fortunate, just like you, in a way. We were helped by the government and by the Jewish community of Hartford. Since that time, my mother and I made our home here. Of course, I had to leave a few times. I spent two years in the army, and a few years studying engineering at 'Rensselaer Polytechnic Institute,' in Upstate New York. But I always came back home."

We pulled into an industrial park and followed the road weaving between concrete buildings. The car stopped in front of one of them. I got out. A large concrete slab with the name *"Wieber Scientific Products"* stood prominently on the front lawn. *"That's pretty odd."* I thought. *"I believe he said that his name was Joe Wieber... Unless I mixed it all up with my poor English. Why his name would be on that rock?"*

We entered the lobby. The receptionist jumped up, cheerfully greeting *"Mr. Wieber"* with her smiley good-morning. Joe nodded and proceeded forward, I followed behind. It seemed that we walked the entire length of the building before entering a large brightly-lit room.

"I thought that before we started it wouldn't hurt to have a cup of coffee and a bite to eat. I have a suspicion that you didn't have a crumb in your mouth since yesterday. My treat!"

It was getting close to lunchtime and the place began filling up. I noticed that every new person entering the room made sure to greet Mr. Wieber. Some came to our table for a small talk. We were on our coffee already when Joseph waved to a heavy set man with a tray in his hands. The man just left the food counter and was searching for a place to land. He grinned and walked over. Joseph introduced me. After the man settled and had a few bites, they went on discussing some production issues. It seemed that the man wasn't comfortable. Finally, he took a big gulp of Coke and complained about designers and engineers who couldn't keep up with modifications asked by the production. After he finished, he gulped the rest of his Coke, and was ready to leave,

"By the way, I am thinking to hire this young man, but don't know yet what department could use him, and most importantly, where he would fit in as an engineer."

Although I didn't understand most of their conversation, it got my attention after I heard the word *"hire."* The man asked me to come by his office after I will be done with Mr. Wieber. *"What did he mean? Will be done with Mr. Wieber… It sounded menacing."* I had no idea. We finished our food and I followed Joseph along long corridors. We stopped in a few rooms where engineers worked on electronic circuitries and some mechanical devices. Finally, we arrived in a spacious office where a young secretary greeted Joseph with a small pile of telephone messages written on pink forms with black header "While you were out…" Joseph grabbed them and waved me to follow him in his private office. Then he excused himself and started dialing. After an hour, he finally remembered that I was still in the room. Someone knocked on the door, and a young lady entered.

"Hi Josie, glad you could come on such short notice."

Joseph went around his desk and kissed the lady on the cheek. Then he turned to me,

"This is Josephine, my good friend's daughter. She goes to *UConn,* her junior year. Guess what?"

He glanced as if getting ready to present me with a surprise. I was surprised alright, not knowing what UConn meant.

"Her second major is the Russian language and literature. She will help us to talk to you."

I didn't get a half of what Joseph said, but as soon as Josie started speaking Russian I felt a lot better. Her language was archaic and heavy-accented, but quite proficient. It seemed that her teachers froze in time sixty years ago and never adapted to modern language. I wasn't too far from the truth. Later on, I met some of them. They had left Russia at the time of the October Communist Revolution of 1917. One thing was clear, Josie was very much ahead in her advancement in Russian than me in English.

It was dark outside when we finished. Joseph insisted that we went out to dinner, and I stayed in a nearby small country inn that night. Visitors to his company said they always enjoyed their stay over there. His secretary had made all the arrangements already. I just needed to show up and tell them my name.

He handed my university transcripts and diploma to Josie, hoping she could make sense out of what I had studied. The documents had been translated into English already by the Immigration assistance people. I had no idea though if they had made an accurate translation. The engineering language was complicated. Joseph asked Josie to go in the morning to her university's engineering department and find out what credentials I had. They would try to figure out what I knew, but mainly, what I didn't know. We agreed to meet again in Joseph's office in the afternoon of the following day.

We had dinner in a restaurant on a tiny river. The restaurant was a watermill in its previous life. Now it was a cozy place to relax by the running water and a crackling fireplace. Josie volunteered to drop me off at the hotel. Joseph didn't object. It looked like he could use some rest. He excused himself and quickly left. We spent another hour at the table when Josie suggested going to a disco which many of her student-friends frequented. The night was still young.

The next morning, I woke up early, excited about the upcoming day. Josie was peacefully sleeping on the other side of the bed. Her Russian might be old-fashioned, but she wasn't old-fashioned in bed at all. I suppose she could teach me a trick or two. Especially, if we were helped by a few joints, she introduced me to. I still could feel their effect, once I got out the bed. I went to a large window and stood there watching the sun rising over the fields covered with thick fog. I didn't hear when Josie quietly slipped off the bed and hugged me from behind,

"Hey buddy, today is a big day! Are you ready? Uncle Joe is a great man. Stick with him, you would never regret." She smiled and added, "Remember, we have a meeting with him today in the afternoon. We have to hurry up."

We had a quick breakfast in the hotel (included in the stay), and hit the road toward a mysterious UConn. I thought I ended up in a dog pound, not on a university grounds. A pack of students dressed as Siberian Huskies was roaming green lawns. They stopped cars, jumping in front of them, and banged on the hood and windows.

"Don't pay any attention to those nuts. The basketball season is starting in a month, but they are already going crazy wearing these husky heads and disgusting fur over their sorry asses."

Josie waved at them to clear the road, to no effect. The wild huskies continued dancing around and shaking the car. In the next moment, I got an opportunity to learn my first authentic American expression. *"Get the f*ck out of my way, you motherf*ckers!"* Josie screamed a few times until it settled firmly in my head. The dogs kept blocking the road. I got out of the car carrying a bat, I conveniently picked up from the back seat. Later on, I learned that smart girls carried a bat in their car, just in case. But even smarter girls had a gun. The dogs seemed to back off, but still stood on the road. It was a perfect moment to exercise my newly acquired knowledge. I barked it a few times to make sure they understood my accent. They did.

Storrs campus of The School of Engineering had sprawling grounds. It took us a while before we reached an old red-brick administration building.

"I called yesterday. My former boyfriend is an engineering student here. He did some legwork for us so we can see a right woman. She is waiting. Those furry bastards slowed us down. Hope she's still there."

She grabbed my hand and pulled me inside the building. We raced up the stairs to the third floor and ran into an office. The woman was still there. We spent the next two hours reviewing my credentials, as they called my Soviet university transcripts. Josie was of a great help. It turned out that it was worth every effort to get good grades. *"The math is the math, and the mathematics is inarguable everywhere, whether it is in Russia, Africa or in America. So goes for Physics. The gravity pulls every ass down with the same forth, whether it is a communist ass or a not so much. The only people who keep arguing against the laws of Physics are either the Marxists or the American Democrats (that I will learn much later)."* While I was praising myself, Josie was feverishly scribbling on a piece of paper, taking notes for Joseph. Finally, she finished, swept all my papers in a large envelope and shook the woman's hand. I did the same.

That time, the road was clear from the mad huskies. Josie was in a good mood,

"You are lucky. The woman said you are an electrical engineer with a few minor deficiencies."

I had no idea what that big word meant, but it sounded intimidating. Josie tried to explain to me in Russian. By the time we made back to the hotel, I got the picture. We still had two hours before meeting with Joseph. We spent the time in bed. Things were looking up. Josie was sleeping naked, spread across my bed. Her breasts were perked and moving with her breathing. *"If I told my college buddies back in Russia that I slept with an American girl, they would've thought I was out of my mind. I would've loved to see their faces now."*

I kept staring at her assessing my new friend, or *"how did they call it...? A girlfriend?"* I didn't know exactly what that word meant. She mentioned that her former boyfriend arranged our meeting that morning. I suppose that implied that she stopped doing with him something they were doing before. *"Perhaps, I have become her new boyfriend... It is too confusing. I'd better stay a f*ck-buddy with her for now. Besides, she is not exactly my type. Although I had not fully defined 'my type' yet."*

Josie was about twenty, junior in college, majoring in business. She was about five-ten and of a slender complexion. She had a round face but proportional with her slim body, and with big blue eyes. Her hay-color hair was cut short, exposing gentle earlobes with small diamond studs. Josie had sensitive lips, slightly open and exposing snow-white sparkling teeth. I suppose that was what they called in America a Hollywood smile. I kept following her down with my eyes. Her neck was smooth and in a perfect proportion with her body. I dwelled again on her breasts moving up and down slightly, and stopped at her stomach. It was flat, without any indication that there were deposits of the fat. I was about to move lower, but she murmured in her sleep and turned over on her stomach. I didn't notice before she had a small tattoo just above her buttocks. It was a strange symbol, of an Oriental nature perhaps. I came closer to take a better look. I was so emerged in studying it, that I didn't realize she turned her head up and was staring at me. Then she quickly turned over, grabbed my head with both hands and stuck my face between her legs. I had never been down that road before. It seemed strange but didn't smell like I imagined. Apparently, Josie didn't want to wait for something to happen and started moving her body rubbing against my nose. The whole area was cleanly shaved, except for a tiny vertical sliver surrounding the lips. Tiny hairline was the same color as her hay-hair. They were tickling my nose until I couldn't hold and sneezed. "Stick your tongue in, silly." Josie was laughing. *I have to taste it, too?"* ran through my head, but obeyed. It didn't taste bad. "Oh…, Oh…, feels so good. C'mon move it!" Josie almost ordered, enjoying herself and speeding up her gyrations. Suddenly, she stopped, pulled away, exposing my tongue hanging out. Then quickly moved to the edge of the bed and pulled me inside her.

We had just a half an hour before our meeting. I was hungry.

"I thought you ate enough pussy to keep you going," Josie laughed getting out of the shower. "Let's run. We get a slice of pizza on the way."

In the car, I was thinking about that thing she said about *"eating pussy…"* Interesting expression. I must remember it and tell someone when they get hungry, I suppose. On the other hand, eating it didn't help me with my hunger, but two slices of pizza with pepperoni did. How bizarre… Deep in these thoughts, we pulled in front of *"Wieber Scientific Products"*. It was two in the afternoon on the dot, as Josie put it. *"I have to start writing all these expressions down,"* I thought.

Joseph was in his office talking on the phone. He pointed to a few chairs around an oval table. He seemed rested. When he hung up, he walked around his large desk and came over to kiss Josie on the cheek and shake my hand. After a small talk about the weather, we settled around the table to report on our findings at UConn. Josie did a good job taking meticulous notes of what the woman at the University's Engineering Department was talking about. The phone rang, and the secretary announced through the speaker that *"they were ready for us."*

"You guys go now. I'd like you to have a chat with my head of the R&D. I'll take another look at your credentials and make a few phone calls. See you in an hour." Joseph got up and quickly moved behind his desk.

While we were walking along a long corridor, Josie realized that I had no clue what R&D meant.

"In case you wonder where we are heading," she smiled, "this is where all the magic happens. People want things that don't exist. Someone has to come up with them. Uncle Joe and his boys invent things and develop them into something they can sell. They build prototypes and test to see if they are any good to start production. It is all about business. By the way, this is where I come in with my future degree."

We walked into a large section of the building hidden behind an inconspicuous door with a small sign *"Research and Development. Authorized Personnel Only."* Some areas were caged with a tall metal fence and covered with white fabric, so you couldn't see what was behind it. A young man showed us to an office where we were greeted by a short, balding man in his thirties. He wore large spectacles, constantly sliding down his nose. With Josie's help, he explained what kind of stuff the company worked on.

Another man came in. He headed straight to the desk, sat on the very edge of it with one foot on the floor and stared at me. He was introduced as a chief engineer of the *Testing and Quality Control Department.* Without his seal of approval, nothing would ever get into production. Nothing would be sold, and no money could be made to keep the company in business. The man's other leg kept swinging like a pendulum taking away my attention and not letting concentrate on his words. I was glued to it. In spite of that destruction, Josie did a great job relaying to me in Russian what the man said.

*****

"So? Do you want the job in Italy?" He was waiting for my answer. "I suppose I have to give you a day or two to think it over. But don't take too long. I need your answer by the next Monday. If you decided to go, you would need to leave as soon as possible. How do they say it in Italy: Capisce…?"

I walked out of his office still seeing in my eyes the hideous argyle of his high socks.

*****

2. "The POND" Is My Home

We returned to Joseph's office and sat again around the oval table. He was expecting us,

"Well, my young friend, I think I have bad and good news for you."

Josie translated. Apparently, she couldn't capture the essence of that expression right. My face turned pale, scaring them that I was going to faint. Joseph rushed to me with a glass of water and hurried with the explanation.

"Please, forgive me, I didn't mean to scare you, but that brings me to the very important point — the English language."

He made sure now that he selected every word carefully.

"Based on the documents you presented this morning to UConn people, you are short a few credits to satisfy the Master of Engineering degree. That is great news, of course. Those few courses you can finish in one year without any sweat. The problem is that you cannot do it without passing the English course first. That I consider bad news."

He looked at Josie,

"Darling, try to explain it to our young friend without scaring him to death."

"Now," Joseph continued, "from here on, it is good news all the way! I think we can offer you a job in R&D," he winked at Josie, sure that I got the explanation already. "We can't hire you as an engineer without your finishing your degree first, but we give you a job of a technician with engineering responsibilities, and pay you as a junior engineer." He smiled. "The news is getting better. My company has a program to pay for the employees' education. That should cover your tuition. If you decide to take the job, our Personnel department will explain."

He leaned back in his chair and grinned. I was sitting there numb, afraid to say anything. *"Of course, I want this job! Any job here! I love it already,"* raced through my head.

"You can think about it for a few days. I tell you what. Yom Kippur, the Day of Atonement is the next week. I'd like you to spend it here. Josie's family goes to a different temple. You are free to choose to spend it with my family, or at Josie's, or both. Even if you decided not to take my offer, I'd still like you to come spend the Holiday here. Josie volunteered to drop you at the rail station in Hartford. It is easier to get back to New York from there." He got up and stretched out his hand. "It is a great pleasure..."

I didn't let him finish, "I take the job!"

It seemed that Joseph wasn't surprised, and even expected my response. He was two steps ahead of me. He turned to Josie,

"I spoke to your dad last night. He came up with an excellent idea, I think. Your Nana's sister owns a large estate in Mansfield. Doesn't she?"

"That was my favorite place in the summertime when I was a child," Josie smiled. "Some people don't have a nana, at all. I have two. I am so lucky."

"Josie, would you mind taking your friend to visit her. She is expecting you both."

Josie seemed surprised but agreed. I had no idea what they were talking about. Most of it I didn't understand, anyway. My mind was racing in a different direction. I had to figure out how to move to Connecticut and find a place to live. As it turned out, Joseph was not two steps, but all ten ahead of me already.

"Great!" He turned to me, "If you need to stay another night or two in the Inn, it is no problem." Then he turned back to Josie, "Send my regards to your Nana's sister." And again, back to me, "This is for you, my young friend…"

Joseph handed me a large notebook with a leather cover, got up and walked us to the door. I had never held such a beautiful thing in my hands. The leather was dark-brown and soft, with *"Wieber Scientific Products"* embossed in gold on it. It seemed that Josie was happy. Whether it was because we were on the way to see her favorite Nana or that she could spend another night with me. We drove on the highway east for a few exits. Once we got off it, the road became narrow and cut through the thick woods. Josie kept silent, seemingly concentrating on her driving. I took out the notebook Joseph gave me. I opened the cover and stared at the blank page. A ballpoint pen was neatly tucked inside the binder. *"Eat pussy…,"* I wrote in the first line. It seemed like a good start to learning American slang. The second line I entered, remembering our arrival to Joseph's office, *"It was two in the afternoon on the dot."* I thought I had another pearl to enter, but we had arrived at our destination.

The car rolled through the remains of a brick gates, and on a narrow but paved road. An old wooden split-rail fence spread out on both sides of the gates. The gates and the fence were just a formality now, not protecting anything from anyone, a stray cow, perhaps. Josie stopped the car in front of an old house with a large front porch. She jumped out and ran through the gravel driveway to the steps leading up. I saw her hugging two older women. Then, as if remembering, she pointed to the car and started waving at me to come in.

The first thing I noticed climbing up the stairs was an old traditional Russian *Samovar*. The name literally translates as a device that boils water by itself. Indeed, it was a self-contained large copper pot to boil water for tea. In the old times, they used wood chips or even chunks of coal to heat it. Nowadays, it was electric. On top, it had a small matching pot to brew strong tea that later was poured into cups and the hot water from the main contraption added to it. *"How odd... In the middle of nowhere in America..."*

Two women in their sixties got up from the rocking chairs to greet me. After a brief introduction, one of them, Nana Rachel, as Josie called her, briefly disappeared and returned with fine porcelain cups on small saucers and with silver teaspoons. Josie introduced the other woman as Ms. Golubov, her college professor of Russian language and literature. I suppose that explained the Samovar presence on the table. Immediately, Josie insisted that we converse in Russian. After a few polite exchanges, it seemed inappropriate to exclude Nana Rachel from the conversation.

We settled around a large oval table to have a *"British five-o'clock tea,"* as Ms. Golubov called it. It was already past six, but the tea was indeed British. The label on a tin can said *"Twinings."* Ms. Golubov noticed me studying the can, and said,

"Do you know, my young friend, that 'Twinings' is the world's oldest used company name. They had started as a tearoom in London's neighborhood called the Strand. The company occupies the same building since 1706 and is the longest taxpayer into the British crown. Imagine, how much dough they shelled out in almost three hundred years…"

Josie started to cheerfully recount the events of the last two days. I used the opportunity to study our hostess and her friend. They were dressed in similar tweed jackets over long, almost to the ground, dark skirts. Underneath jackets, they both wore light-beige blouses with similar silver brooches tightly holding collars around their neck. Nana Rachel's brooch stone matched the color of her blue eyes. Ms. Golubov had a green stone in her brooch, contrasting with her gray eyes. Nana Rachel had a round face, quite similar to Josie's. They were relatives, after all. Her head was still full of curly, but gray hair. She had smooth olive skin and small tightly closed lips with a heavy layer of a red lipstick. Her nose was small. When she spoke, she exposed two accurate rows of white teeth. They looked like they were still her own. Ms. Golubov was taller of the two. She was slimmer and had a horse head, usually found on British women. Her hair was a former blond, but with a lot of gray. She had a large forehead of a scholar, and small beady eyes, drilling a person with a penetrating look. I wouldn't want to be her student, for sure. When she spoke, I could see that her teeth were all in place, but not as white as her friend's. Ms. Golubov had a long, pointy nose over small, colorless lips. If I didn't know, I could've mistaken them for two sisters, perhaps…

If Josie didn't drag me from the table under a legitimate excuse to show the grounds, god only knows what other conclusions I could've arrived to. We crossed the back lawn and took a narrow path through the woods. It was a large estate, to say the least. In a few minutes, we found ourselves standing by a small cottage overlooking a pond. The sun started to set down. It was an early fall, but the trees were still full of leaves just starting to change color and blocking the last golden rays.

"Hurry up before the darkness falls. We can still catch the ride."

Josie pulled me to a small boat and jumped into it without any hesitation. I followed. We rowed around the pond with her reminiscing about great times she spent on the estate.

"See that cottage? I used to live there every summer since I was ten. Now, if you like, Nana Rachel agreed that you can have it."

I didn't get it and was looking at her with a stupid grin. She tried again,

"It is fifteen minutes from the University campus. You can ride a bike from here. But Nana Rachel said you could use her old 'Chevy' to get around. She has another car for herself. She was actually excited that there will be another person on the property besides deer and wild boars. I suppose you could help her with some chores, too."

It was a dollhouse, but it had it all. Two rooms had been converted into bedrooms. Adjacent to them was a tiny kitchen and a bathroom, even with a tub. A small wood-burning stove stood in the corner of one of the rooms.

"Why don't we stay here tonight instead of the Inn. I will run to tell Nana Rachel that you are going to test your new digs. You will announce your decision tomorrow morning. By the way, I had lost my virginity in the next room..."

She giggled and disappeared even before I could understand everything she said. I looked around. *"Everything seemed to fall in its place. I got a job. I got the place to live. I got the school to finish my degree. I even got a girl. It seemed like a fairy tale... It all happened so fast."* Josie was back soon. We got in her car and drove into the nearby town. It seemed she knew all the hot places and a lot of people. It was her college town. Every kid wanted to talk to me, and even touch me as if I was an exotic animal from the Bronx Zoo.

It amazed me that the Americans knew so little about what was going on in Europe, and even less in the Soviet Union. We were in the midst of the Cold War. Of course, they heard about the Soviet refugees and how hard it was to find the way out of the Soviet Union. Some kids knew bits and pieces about their ancestors from random Eastern European countries, but that knowledge didn't go too far. Meeting someone alive and well from behind the Iron Curtain was beyond their imagination. People were fascinated with my journey. That night, I was the center of attention and endless toasts to my new-found freedom.

We returned to "my cottage" just as the first streaks of dawn showed above the horizon, but stayed awake for another hour. Finally, exhausted, we fell asleep. I woke up to the sun piercing through the window. Josie murmured something, and kicked her blanket off the bed, exposing her naked body lying on her stomach. I crawled closer to look at her tattoo above the buttocks. That time, I intended to find out about it. She murmured again and turned on her back spreading her legs like a pair of open scissors. I kept staring at her until she opened her eyes.

"What?" She smelled of last night's alcohol. "Don't worry, it was in another room," she pointed to the wall. "I mean my virginity…"

Honestly, I forgot about it with all the drinking last night, but said,

"That symbol on your butt… You know, Jews don't approve of any things added to the perfect body God once created."

"Nonsense!" Josie woke up suddenly. "Jews don't approve of a lot of things. One of them, I am about to do to you." She quickly grabbed my penis with her mouth.

"Hold on! Hold on! I wanted to ask you something."

It had to wait till later.… I was still determined to find out about her tattoo. Josie got to it first,

"You were wondering about the symbol on my back…
I suppose I can tell you. A few years ago, when I was a freshman in college, I went to Israel with a group of students for a couple of weeks. It felt great to get away from our winter in January. They drove us around the country, told about their history, and even tried to teach a few words. I don't remember much, but a few letters stuck in my head. To my surprise, our professor of Russian studies Ms. Golubov mentioned in her lectures the complexity of the Russian language, comparing it to the Chinese for a foreigner who started studying it. A few times, she drew on the blackboard some Chinese symbols. One of them caught my eye. It stood for life, fate, and destiny.

A bizarre thing about it was that two Hebrew characters were sitting 'under the roof' of that symbol, reflecting the entire meaning of it.

ק The letter *Koof* of Hebrew alphabet equals the number one hundred, signifying the completion of the living matter. It is said that at the age of one hundred a person returns to the dust from which they came.

ס The letter *Sameh* is a closed form. It is symbolic of the endless cycle of life. It is a symbol of support and protection. I was so fascinated with that mystique that when a bunch of my girlfriends talked me into going to a tattoo parlor, I had a clear design in my head already."

We stayed in bed till Nana Rachel came looking for us. She prepared breakfast. We sat on the front porch eating a country omelet and listening to the morning birds chirping away in the woods. Later that afternoon, I picked up my only bag from an apartment in Brooklyn, where I was temporarily rooming with some immigrants. I wished them to have a nice life and took off to start my own in my new country.

*****

3. **Nana Got A Gun**

I felt that I had to be at Joseph's temple for the Yom Kippur services. Josie didn't object, but "gently suggested" that it would be beneficial to visit her temple, too, and thank her dad for all the good things that happened to me. She was right, but somehow I resisted meeting her family just yet. I didn't fully understand all the implications of becoming a boyfriend. I was fine to be just a friend. I had too much on my plate at the moment.

Everything turned out to be less intense than I imagined. I suppose it was because of the seriousness of the holiday. The prayers went along, and the rabbi did his sermon. Then some people went up in front to say their prayers. Finally, Joseph came forward and read a tribute to his father, who had perished in a concentration camp forty years ago. He briefly recounted his own salvation this great country had extended to him and his mother. He promised never to forget the kindness of the people and repay them with anything he could, including helping the immigrants. After Joseph's speech, we shook hands with him and the rabbi. It seemed that we had fulfilled our obligations there, and hurried to meet Josie's folks at another temple in Farmington.

It was my first ever celebration of the Day of Atonement. I always thought that the Christians could get forgiveness for their sins. At least, that was how it was presented in the Soviet Union. *"You sin around all you want. Then go to a confession and the priest makes you whole, to start sinning again. Don't forget the donation, otherwise, all bets are off. You will burn in hell."*

Apparently, Jews didn't have the luxury of shedding their sins off on a regular basis, or *"play for pay,"* as Josie put it.

(I entered that expression in the next line of my notebook.)
I suppose there was some rationale for it. I didn't know about ancient times, but nowadays, who had time to confess often? Just look at me. Every day, I got up at six in the morning. It was still warm enough to take a quick dip in the lake before heading to my new job. Josie and Nana Rachel thought that I was crazy to swim in the ice-cold water. I assured them that it was a normal water temperature in the summer where I came from. A few Josie's college friends tried to swim with me last weekend, but if not for a few weed joints and shots of tequila they wouldn't do it... After work, I rushed to the campus to take my *"English as a Second Language Class,"* which usually extended to more than two hours. After a bite to eat, I would head back to my cottage to fall exhausted in bed. If I found Josie there, we would enjoy ourselves for a while, sometimes a long while, till it was six o'clock and time to jump in the lake again.

I felt Josie's elbow gently pushing into my side and her whispering in my ear,

"Go, go on... They don't bite!" Josie was grinning. "Go up front, silly. The rabbi called you. It is the highest honor."

I had no idea what the rabbi possibly wanted with me. I didn't speak any language he or the audience could understand but got up. I made my way up front and climbed onto the podium near the rabbi. The temple was full, overflowing with people. It looked intimidating. I had never spoken in front of so many people before, especially in a foreign language. I guess the rabbi had better things in mind for me to do than speaking. He put a white shawl over my shoulders and asked everyone to join him in a prayer for the Soviet Jews. He took my hand in his. His hand was small and warm and immediately reminded me of my Grandmother Dora's I always remembered, although she had not been with us for a few years already.

The rabbi closed his eyes and spoke in the depth of the temple. His words floated above everyone's head and went up. From there, his words had nowhere to go but straight to God. Many people closed their eyes in silent devotion. *"Were they really praying, or just tired, and closed their eyes to rest for a moment? Probably praying...,"* I concluded. When the rabbi was done, he asked everyone to join him for the evening services. Then he wished to all a good fasting. I was glad it was over. We packed Nana Rachel in the car and headed to our pond in the woods.

A few days before, I came to the office for the first time. I went straight to the Personnel Department. It was all new to me. I had to fill out a gazillion forms that I couldn't even understand. I took them back home (*yes, I had home already!*). With Josie and Nana Rachel's help, I was able to labor through them. One form, in particular, grabbed my attention. The company would guarantee my tuition to finish my Master's degree at UConn School of Engineering for as long as I agreed to commit to work for the company for at least two years after the graduation. To me, it seemed as a no-brainer *(the word went straight into my expressions notebook)*. Nana Rachel agreed with me, too. But Josie... Josie went off the cliff (*that was another expression I learned that night*).

"How Uncle Joseph could do it to the people. They are not his slaves. True, he pays for their school, but two years... Give me a break!"

That last one was a beauty, too, and deserved a big entrée in my notebook. I would be soon running out of pages, hanging around Josie. So far I had not found anything worthwhile from my English classes at the University to enter in there. I had to learn a lot more about Josie. Looked like she was a free spirit. I thought that two years weren't that bad to work off thirty grand Joseph would spend on my degree. Besides, I might like the job and stick around longer. Josie didn't want to hear it. That night, she went home to sleep. Later on, I heard that she had given Joseph a hard time on every occasion she could. It was inconceivable to me that someone wanted to give that gentleman hard time for all good things he had done in his life. Everything passes. That cloud passed, too.

The following spring, I had my first graduation. After two grueling semesters of studying English at the university every night, learning a technical language every day in the office, and scribbling in my notebook of expressions the pearls I picked from Josie, her friends, and on the street, I felt that I was ready to be an American. We celebrated the English credits towards my Master's degree in an old two-storey pub right off the Interstate 84 in the downtown of Hartford. When every toast was raised and everyone was sufficiently drunk, I pulled out my notebook. It became twice as thick from the original Joseph had gifted me with. The leather on top was worn out. I opened it up and started reading from the top. My first line was about *"eating pussy…"* Behind every expression I entered was a story. My real graduation and the Master of Electrical Engineering degree had arrived a year later.

Josie was graduating that same spring. We decided to have our party together. Nana Rachel offered to host it in her estate. She arranged for a large tent on the front lawn and caterers bringing food and drinks. It was the Memorial Day weekend, almost summer already. When the last guest was gone, it was Nana Rachel with her friend Professor Golubov left sitting on the porch. It was an early evening and the gentle sunset put a golden color on surrounding woods.

Josie, fresh from running back from the gates, seeing off the last guests, landed on the chair next to me. She was excited and heavy breathing.

"Nana Rachel, you never told how you ladies ever met, and yet, I see you together for as long as I remember."

"You never asked, darling. It is about time. Regardless, we met through 'The Samuel Clemens Society.' Do you know who Samuel Clemens was?"

She stared at me, rightly assuming that I was the one to ask. I didn't think I heard that name before. The ladies looked surprised. Nana Rachel glanced at **Professor** Golubov as if it was her fault for my poor education, but continued,

"Does Mark Twain sound more familiar, perhaps? Anyway, my late husband and I were active in turning the Mark Twain's house in Hartford into a museum. Ms. Golubov came one night to the Society meeting. She had just moved in the area to teach Russian at the UConn and was lonely. Naturally, she found her way to Mark Twain's museum. We became friends. Although in the beginning, we had some difficulties communicating," she glanced at me again, "we still could share beautiful literature. She taught me about Pushkin, Turgenev, and many other great Russians, we know so little about in this country. When my husband passed away, I made sure to move closer to my friend. I bought this estate, 'The Pond,' from an old recluse. And here we are, sitting on this porch under the starry heavens."

The sun had gone down and the long shadows blanketed the house. I excused myself and ran to my cottage to refresh. I was about to get out of the door and get on my way back to the main house when the phone rang. *"Strange...,"* I thought, *"we just saw everyone at the party,"* but picked the receiver. I heard a heavy breathing on the other end,

"Please, don't panic," Nana Rachel whispered. "Listen carefully and do exactly as I say."

"Are you okay?" I hurriedly whispered back.

"No! I am not okay! But please do what I say." She stopped for a second. Everything was quiet on the other end. "Come to the house through the back door in the den. Grab a rifle from the wall. It is loaded with a cartridge. You will have five bullets."

I had to stop her,

"I have no idea how to use it, Nana Rachel. I may hurt someone by accident."

"Shoot…," I heard her whispering, clearly disappointed.

"Shoot who?"

"Not who, but whom," she couldn't help but correct me. "Put it in your notebook." She paused for another second. "All right then, grab a hunting knife on the wall instead, but tuck it in your pants. Hide it in your back. Do not cut yourself, please. Then go around the house to the front porch, go slow. Don't freak out! There will be a man standing by Josie holding a knife to her throat." I could hear, she swallowed a lump. "When the man would go after you, run as fast as you can to the front gates. I know you are a good runner. This time, you must run for your life. Hopefully, the cops will be there already. I will do the rest. Now hang up, call the police, and go."

I dialed the police. Trying to stay as calm as I could muster, I explained in a trembling voice what Nana Rachel wanted me to do. They ordered me to stay put and do not go to the main house under any circumstances. They were already on the way. It should take them fifteen minutes to get to us. I couldn't wait that long knowing that I could help. I carefully went around the main house, making sure not to step on twigs. Holding my breath, I gently pried the back door with my both hands trying not to make it squeak. Just as Nana Rachel said, I found a rifle on the wall. It was loaded with a cartridge sticking from under the barrel. A large hunting knife was on the wall next to it. I removed it from the holster and tried to stick in my waistband behind my back. I felt a cold blade touching my buttocks. It felt uncomfortable. I moved it around, but couldn't get the twelve-inch blade fit. Then it occurred to me that I could fasten the holster holding the knife to my leg. It worked. I even could run with it.

Once again, I gently got the door open and carefully went around the house. I saw the back of the man standing on the porch next to a chair. Josie was sitting in it. It was too high to jump the man from behind. I started around the house, as Nana Rachel said, not to scare the man by my sudden appearance. It worked. I was twenty feet in front of the porch when I heard Nana Rachel saying calmly to the man,

"Leave the girl alone now. Didn't you come for this man?" She pointed to me.

I had no idea what to expect, but drew the blade out of the holster. I felt that it would be easier for me to run, too. Apparently, it produced the effect Nana Rachel was hoping for. The man stepped away from Josie. I could see her eyes filled with fear, but she was calm. Her hands were tied together with a rope in the back of the chair. The man made two more steps towards the porch rail. It appeared that he wanted to take a closer look at me. At that very moment, I heard a single gunshot. The man took one more step forward and rolled down the steps, hitting every one of them with his head.

"Move away, young man," I heard Nana Rachel's firm voice. "You've done your job perfectly"

At that moment, I saw two police cars racing up the driveway in the cloud of dust. They stopped in front of the house. The cops jumped out with their guns drawn, hiding behind the wide-open car doors. The man lay on the ground motionless. Nana Rachel still held the barrel over the man's head. Then she slowly put it on the ground, raised her arms up, and said a loud prayer, first in Hebrew, then in English. Professor

Golubov was busy trying to set Josie free. Then they both ran to Nana Rachel and embraced.

Nana Rachel seemed very composed and calm as if she didn't shoot a man just a few minutes ago. The police had "secured the suspect, " as I heard them talking over their radios. There was nothing to secure – the man seemed pretty dead. First, an ambulance arrived to pick up the injured. Nana Rachel was a serious woman and took care of business, leaving no injured behind. They retreated quickly, clearing room for the County Coroner's van. The body was removed. After hugging her friend and Josie, she stepped back and sat in her armchair. The police people took a deposition from every one of us. No charges had been filed against Nana Rachel citing self-defense and protection of lives and private property. It was a legal parlance, I had learned later on. As soon as the police left, Josie's parents arrived, followed by Joseph. Then other family members came, then friends, and the friends of the friends with casual onlookers in tow. Finally, a local radio and TV station showed up. Somehow, Nana Rachel managed to ask the police to stick around and protect the privacy of the residence. They did their job, blocking the road to the estate against curious passers-by. The only people they had let through were the three National Network News. Nana Rachel agreed to be interviewed.

Overnight, all three major networks put up their tents on the front lawn. The following morning, Nana Rachel was seated on the porch in her armchair with the rifle casually leaning against its side. They ran down the list of usual opening questions. Then one of the correspondents asked,

"Who was the culprit you so bravely took down and freed the hostages? Did you know him?"

"Well," Nana Rachel paused, as if considering whether to answer the question, but said, " he was a local young man, a college student of Engineering. My granddaughter had dated him for a while. Then they went their own ways. It happens every day. People get together, then split, get back again… Unfortunately, something happened to him."

"Ma'am, you took him down with one shot! It is remarkable, considering that it started to get dark, and you had to get your gun out of hiding and shoot fast. Where did you learn the skill?"

"I have to thank my late husband Abe, G-d bless his soul." Nana Rachel sighed deeply. "All his life, he was in the commercial insurance business. Among his many clients, he had a few gun manufacturers. Most insurers shied away from that business, but he embraced it. His most favorite was 'Colt's Manufacturing Company.' They were local boys from Hartford. Then, there was another one, he liked — 'Sturm-Ruger Company,' down in Southport. This rifle that did the job so magnificently was the Colt's ArmaLite AR-15." She took it in her arms and petted as a favorite cat. "This one is the predecessor of the military M16 rifle that saved so many of our boys overseas."

The news people tried to switch to some personal questions, but Nana Rachel was determined to finish what she started.

"Don't take me wrong, people. I have some other beauties downstairs. Ruger could've done the job just as well." The correspondent tried to stop the cameraman, discreetly showing to cut the interview off. He didn't know Nana Rachel yet. "My husband loved Ruger. He picked that company up just as they opened their doors in 1949. They stayed with him ever since. Everyone knows Ruger for their pistols. I must assure you folks, their 'Deerstalker' rifle is a great gun, too." She looked at me, " I told this boy to grab it. I loaded it with the magazine for him. Too bad, nowadays, young people don't know how to handle a good gun…" She sighed again, and kept talking, "I have a couple of Winchesters…"

This time, the newsman stopped her and politely asked where she learned to shoot. He should've thought twice.

"I was afraid of guns. When Abe told me about his new customers, I was terrified. Then one day, he talked me into going with him to visit the Rugers boys. We had a pleasant lunch in their offices overlooking Long Island sound. Then they offered to show us their new toys. It seemed that my Abe wasn't a stranger to that exercise. He went out and returned, dressed in military fatigues. He carried another set for me. I looked awful…, dressed like a little soldier. Thank G-d, my lady-friends didn't see me then. We took a Jeep to their range. I could tell the men had a lot of fun. I tried, too. I must admit that I liked it. The rest is history. I became a regular at our range in town. Soon, I couldn't believe it, we founded 'The Ladies Gun Club of Connecticut.' "

They were about to wrap it up when Nana Rachel asked to add something else,

"The United States Constitution guarantees the Right to bear arms and protect ourselves. The Second Amendment has just saved my life and the lives of those dear to me folks. The communists on the West coast and the Democrats are trying hard to take our guns away. I urge young people to own guns and learn how to handle them. One day, our own government may turn against us the people!"

Nana Rachel turned to the reporters,

"Don't you even try to edit out my words."

Surprisingly, they didn't. That night, we had watched our brave Nana Rachel on the National news. After the program was over, she got up and turned to me and Josie,

"We will start tomorrow. I have a small range in the woods in the back."

*****

The school was over. My brand-new Engineering degree was pinned to the wall in my cottage. A copy of it was proudly displayed in my office at work. I started enjoying my life. I didn't have to run like crazy after work to college, after college to the cottage, and back to work in the morning. It had been my life for the last two years. All of a sudden, I could get back home and do whatever I wanted to do. I had never had that feeling of freedom before.

Josie, on the other hand, was shuttling between home and Washington, D.C. Finally, they made her an offer. She accepted. The downside was that she had to move to Washington. It seemed that it didn't bother me much. For the past two years, we had been very close. Those were our college years, though. That was an excuse of sorts for not making a move to propose her. Everyone around considered us as a couple already. I had to give Josie a credit, she didn't push. In fact, she never asked. Now we were professionals with jobs and the future. I had to decide what to do about it. When Josie got the job with the State Department, I felt relieved. Perhaps, the pressure of urgency could subside on its own, unless Josie would ask.

I found so much time on my hands that I started doing small handy-work around the property. I discovered that I liked it and could fix many things, saving Nana Rachel some money. It turned out that it was quite a significant amount. I found it when Nana Rachel stopped taking rent from me. I protested at first, then gave up.

I took up a new sport. Some wouldn't call it a sport, but I would. Although the estate was in somewhat shabby condition, Nana Rachel didn't cut corners when she had built her shooting range. She employed one of her late husband's old pals from Colt's. He put his heart in it. The man used a natural landscape when constructing the range. The very back of the property had a steep hill topped with old oaks. They had a part of the hill raised even more with sand, creating a bullet trap area. He put two shooting stands. One was fifty and the other was a hundred yards away from the targets at the foot of the hill. The partition between the stands was made of a clear plastic, so people could see each other. The man was retired and had nothing to do all day long. Perhaps, he had another reason to hang around Nana Rachel, and away from his own wife. Even now, a few years after the range was completed, he still would come on occasion and shoot with us.

I became quite fond of our shooting practices. First, Nana Rachel taught me to shoot a rifle, thinking that I would have a better control. Her husband left her quite an arsenal of weaponry, and a pile of boxes of ammunition. I suppose that we could hold our fort against the commies for some time. She hated the West coast with a passion. She called them the left-coast Hollywood's little shits. Then, the time came for me to learn shooting handguns.

One morning, Nana Rachel came out of the house dressed like a cowboy, I had only seen in the movies. I still remembered the "Magnificent Seven," shown in the Soviet Union when I was in the middle-school. Nana Rachel had on brown leather pants with a belt decorated with shiny metal buttons. Two holsters housed a revolver and a semi-automatic handgun. The rest of the belt was full of bullets stuffed in their little nests. She wore a cream-colored blouse with a leather string tie and a leather Texas-style hat adorned with matching shiny buttons. I didn't have anything of a kind. I had to use my old jeans and a baseball hat from the UConn's lousy team.

Our small procession continued to the range. Nana Rachel marched first, I followed behind, and Professor Golubov brought up the rear. Unlike her friend, she dragged her feet without any enthusiasm, for she was against guns, and violence in general. The way she described herself, she was a pacifist. She was dressed in a long summer dress and a straw hat fitting for a summer picnic. After a short introduction to the handgun history and their mechanical construction, we promptly moved on to the actual shooting.

That summer, we had fun at the Nana Rachel's range. She was a competitive woman. She couldn't pass on an opportunity to show her marksmanship, or shall I say markswomanship... Any time she had someone over, she would challenge that house-guest to a target exercise. Besides usual stationary paper targets, soda cans, and empty bottles, Nana Rachel had a moving wild boar, a jumping rabbit, and a running deer. Her pride and joy was a large brown bear moving towards you, and stopping just short of your shooting stand if you missed him. For a person who didn't know the trick, it looked intimidating. We had a lot of good laughs on that account. After the unfortunate accident that spring, she added some new targets to the range. There was a man with a knife, a man with a handgun, and a man with a rifle. All of them had an uncanny resemblance to the guy she shot dead.

That fall, Nana Rachel and Professor Golubov presented me with a birthday gift. It was a new 9mm *Beretta* handgun. Although Professor Golubov was against guns, she still signed my birthday card and wished me many happy shootings. I suppose it was done under duress, with a little help of Nana Rachel.

*****

4. Ms. Golubov

It seemed that the woods got a tight grip on the only bright spot around the table on the porch. It was still early, but the days got noticeably shorter. It was the first sign that the summer was almost over. Josie was leaving tomorrow for Washington, D.C. to start her first job at The State Department. She invited a few friends over, but they were gone already. It was still early to retire in the cottage. Since the first day I had met Professor Golubov, I was curious about her but never got a chance to talk. That night, Josie beat me to it.

"Ms. Golubov, I wanted to thank you for all you have done for me. There is no price to put on your time and knowledge you have given. Thanks to you, I got my job. I guess you taught me Russian well. They didn't care about my accent, either. Last spring at the job fair, when they came on campus to recruit people, I easily had made the cut. Tomorrow, I am starting a new chapter in my life."

"Don't mention it, Josie. That's my job, darling."

Professor Golubov was too modest. The Russian department at UConn was doing pretty good for the university's enrollment, bringing in many new students every year. Professor Golubov played a big part. Students were seeking her as their professor. Her classes were always full, and the waiting list had never gotten shorter. Besides regular courses, she taught night classes, and in the summertime, she conducted the continuing education program for high school teachers. As if that wasn't enough, she held monthly adult education classes and put together Russian plays in the student theater. I couldn't understand where she found time to do all of that. Professor Golubov was too modest. Meanwhile, Josie asked,

"Professor Golubov, as much as I am sorry to say this, I am no longer your student. Perhaps now, you can allow to ask a personal question..." Josie stared at her with a straight face, "It may sound too intrusive, but why 'Ms.' you like people to use in your name. There is some uncertainty in it, isn't it?"

"You know your English well. I hope people at the State Department will appreciate that too. You are right, all my life has been one big uncertainty." Professor Golubov deeply sighed and shifted in her chair.

"Josie, leave my friend alone," Nana Rachel hurried to her rescue.

"Oh! No! No! This is not a problem. I will tell you a story..." Professor Golubov said.

She got up, filled her and Nana Rachel's cup with fresh tea, and started,

"I was two, maybe three years old. We lived in St. Petersburg when the Russian Revolution broke out in 1917. I was the youngest of three sisters. I remember very little of that time. The only thing I remember was an endless train journey. It probably lasted for a month until we reached the Russian port on the Pacific Ocean, the city of Vladivostok. I could still hear in my head the clickety-clack of the wheels. We had crossed entire Russia, traveling six thousand miles. Later, I was told that my dad had hoped to catch a boat to Shanghai. Somehow it did not work out, and my father took us once again by train to a small Chinese town across the Russian border. We had spent the harsh winter there until the roads became passable. Eventually, we had made back to the coast and took a boat to Shanghai.

I don't remember well our first few years there. I stayed home and was schooled together with my middle sister by our mother. Mama was an educated woman. She and my older sister gave lessons of French and music to wealthy Chinese families.

Papa couldn't find work fitting his education. The best he could get, a counter clerk position at small stores. Money was tight. We had to give up on a lot of things we were used to back in St. Petersburg. Unexpectedly, my older sister got a job at a large fashion store in the Shanghai's French Quarter. She was probably eighteen at the time. Soon things started changing for us for the better. Then one day, my sister announced that she quit her job and went into business for herself. At that time in Shanghai, it was unheard of for a woman to own a business. Somehow, she managed to get it going together with another gal, also a former salesgirl from the fashion store. One thing I remember for sure that anything we needed, we had. Later on, she managed to set me and my sister with jobs in large stores in the French Concession. I had no idea what my older sister did, but she earned good money and could provide for all of us, including Mama and Papa."

Professor Golubov leaned back in her chair, and continued,

"When I turned twenty, my older sister got married to an Italian sea captain. It was a big wedding. I didn't realize, so many people knew her. The ceremony was in a newly-built Russian church in the French Concession. I heard she gave some big money to build that church. Then the war broke out in 1937. The Japanese occupied the city, leaving the French Quarter and the International Settlement area, where many foreigners lived, relatively independent. The rest of the city they turned into ruins. By that time, we moved inside the French Quarter and felt safe. My older sister had an apartment on the *Bund*. That area along the *Huangpu River* was the center of finance and trade. It had the most expensive residential apartment houses in town, mixed with embassies, banks, and fashionable stores. We knew that she too was probably safe, but her husband was on his freighter returning from Europe. He could not sail his ship back in Shanghai. The port was blocked.

One day, I went to see my sister. The apartment was locked. I had a set of keys. She wasn't there. It looked like she had not been there for a few days. All kinds of dark thoughts raced through my mind. I asked around the neighbors. No one had seen her for days. I remember sitting in the apartment till it turned dark, thinking what to tell Mama and Papa. I didn't tell them anything. A few days later, I returned to the apartment. She wasn't there. A few more weeks passed. I kept coming back hoping that one day she would turn up. She never did. She vanished in the thin air.

Meanwhile, we were hearing that the entire world had been going to hell. Europe was engulfed in war. The Americans were fighting the Japanese. The Japanese were fighting the Chinese. The Russians were fighting both, the Germans and the Japanese. We managed to survive protected by the miracle of a few words of the agreement establishing invisible borders of the International Settlement area. It seemed that our small island in the middle of devastated Shanghai was the safest place in the world.

My middle sister was dating a Jewish man working at another store. His family was from Europe and moved to Shanghai as soon as the Nazis came to power in Germany in 1933. They had a garment business, selling fabrics to dress makers. Papa was against it, hoping that some Russian prince would show up one day. He still had two daughters to give away. There were a lot of crooks and swindlers claiming a relation to the deposed Russian Tsar. They all were looking to cash in quick. Every time a Russian 'count' or a 'crown-prince' had disappointed Papa, the less he protested his daughters' choice. Mama gave up a long time ago and was happy if her daughters were.

By the end of the war, I met a young man, who worked in the French Trade Representation in Shanghai. It was a very strange arrangement. The legitimate French government had been deposed by the occupying Germans in 1940. The 'Vichy Government' of the Nazi collaborators had been installed instead. French people in the Shanghai office didn't want to recognize the illegitimate government, but kept coming to work anyway, even though they didn't know who they worked for. The amazing thing was they were still getting paid.

The war had ended when the Americans dropped two atomic bombs on Hiroshima and Nagasaki. It was August of 1945. The Japanese had surrendered. They pulled out of China, leaving a vacuum behind. Not for too long, though. The Chinese communists began gaining power, and with the help of their Russian comrades started taking over. There was nothing to look forward in Shanghai but leave. I was thirty years old. My middle sister and I were married on the same day. It was an elaborate production to assure that everyone concerned was satisfied. My older sister was still well-remembered in the Russian church she helped to build. To make my Papa and Mama happy, we had a modest ceremony there first. Then the entire procession moved into a Jewish temple, where my middle sister and her groom stood under Chuppah and smashed a glass wrapped in a white towel for a long unbroken life together. Jacob's family was happy. Eventually, we made to a French Church, where the remaining French contingent had been made whole. In a way we were lucky. We got three ceremonies for our money, so to speak.

There was another reason for us to hurry up. With the end of the war, Australia opened their door to people displaced from Europe. It was a once in a lifetime opportunity for millions to finally find a home. America was still closed to the European immigrants. It was a no-brainer for my sister and her ex-German husband. He and his family would never go back to Germany. They hated their guts. Surprisingly, Papa and Mama gladly agreed to go together with them to Australia. Their old Tsarist Russian passports had long expired. Through the years, the Soviets kept after them urging to exchange, and threatening to leave them stateless. Indeed, they had been stateless for the past twenty years. The Australians didn't care. Papa' and Mama's passports of the non-existing Russian Empire were good enough for them. At the beginning of 1946, my husband and I saw them off at the Shanghai's port. We didn't go. Instead, we packed our belongings and took a ship around the world to Istanbul. After a few weeks there, we had crossed the Mediterranean to Marseille, France."

Professor Golubov got up from her chair and poured some fresh tea for Nana Rachel and herself, then continued,

"My husband's family was from Paris. Naturally, we went there, just to find that they had abandoned their apartment and spent the war-years in the countryside. They didn't want to return and gave us their apartment facing the Seine River and the Notre-Dame Cathedral on a small island across. My husband went back to work for the Civil Foreign Service leaving me as a housewife at home. Every day, I took long walks, enjoying the City of Lights. Until one day, I wandered into Sorbonne University campus that happened to be just a half-mile away from our apartment. I suppose it was a sign from above. I enrolled in language studies. My husband was very happy that I found something to occupy myself with.

Three years passed. I got proficient in French. My studies had drawn to an end. I had graduated with a degree in Romance languages as the major, and Russian as the minor. It may sound funny that Russian was my minor. At the same time, we had grown apart with my husband. Soon, we got divorced. Perhaps, it was time to begin something new. I decided to turn my life around and went to the American embassy to look at the job postings. UConn had been looking to fill an assistant professor position in the Russian language department. The rest is history, as they say."

"Ms. Golubov, I was wondering what happened to your sisters."

Josie couldn't wait even for a second. I saw the fire in her eyes, I only had seen when we were having sex. I knew she wouldn't let it go, in spite of Nana Rachel's loud protesting to call it a night.

"Well, I keep in touch with my middle sister in Melbourne. After they had settled in Australia, she had three children. Not long ago, Papa has died, but Mama is still doing well. She lives in an elder-assisted community not far from my sister's."

"Ms. Golubov, I don't mean to pry, but have you found your older sister?"

She shook her head, got up, and without saying a word, retired from the porch.

That night, Josie couldn't stop, as if something possessed her. We stayed up making love till the morning. Finally, exhausted, I couldn't move any part of my body and fell asleep still inside her. She giggled and rolled away. When I came to, I saw her sprawled across the bed on her stomach with that Chinese symbol up. *"Now it all makes sense,"* I thought, and quickly went back to sleep. When I opened my eyes, Josie was staring at me. I was about to open my mouth when she put her finger to my lips. She didn't move, but kept staring at me in total silence. Finally, she removed her finger, and I could speak,

"Josephine...? Who names a kid that name, anyway? It sounds from a distant past...,"

I couldn't come up with anything better after a night of a great sex she gifted me with. It was too late. Her face clouded in resentment, but quickly cleared in a small smile,

"My parents always wanted a boy. They even prepared a name. They wanted to call me Joseph after some grandfather who passed away ages ago. Even when I was born, they thought it was a boy first, until they saw of course what they needed to see. They tried for a while to conceive another child but didn't get lucky. So instead of Joseph, they ended up with Josephine."

By the time, we returned to the main house, Nana Rachel was getting ready to serve lunch on the porch. A bottle of *Sherry* was opened and two glasses had some of it.

"Do you, kids, care for some…," Professor Golobov pointed to the bottle. "If you do, you better hurry up. We love this balsam."

*****

5. A Strange Stop In Rome

On Monday morning, I returned to the office, ready to face my boss. I struggled through the entire weekend. It was not an easy decision. Just as my life became almost normal, I had to think about uprooting and getting myself to another place. If only that place was in the U.S, it would've been easy, but in Italy? I was barely five years out of the Soviet Union having lived through the biggest upheaval in my life. I just started getting the hang of the capitalist ways, and enjoying it, too. The offer was too good to dismiss.

"I will go," I said without any preliminaries.

It seemed that I startled him. My boss was sitting at his desk. He lifted his head up and aimlessly stared at me as if trying to recognize who disturbed his morning. Then he put a pen down, walked around the desk and sat on the very corner, as he did last Friday. The socks were still hideous, but the color of the "argyles" had changed to red and green. I didn't realize that Christmas had come early that year. It was summer behind the window.

"Can you leave in two weeks?"

"I would like in three…," I had a good reason to ask for an extra week.

"Done!"

I arrived in The Grand Central Station with the first train out of Hartford. It was already hot on that July 4th. It was much cooler near the water of the New York harbor. Even that early in the morning, there were long lines of tourists to board the boats crossing from the Battery park to the Liberty Island. I found a special line with a red carpet and got in the queue.

An attendant checked my papers, and smiling, cheered me up, *"Good luck, guy! Welcome to America!"*

We were seated at the foot of the Lady Liberty on folding chairs set up in concentric semicircles. A podium with the seal of the US President was set up in front. Two dozen of the American flags created the background behind it. In the back, I could see the TV cameras of the alphabet networks busy training their lenses on the podium. There were two hundred guests invited, and probably just as many security people running the grounds. I sat down and looked around. The only language, I didn't hear was English. People were excited and taking pictures.

A man came to the podium and ceremoniously announced, *"Ladies and Gentlemen, please welcome the President of The United States!"* A military band started playing *"The Star-Spangled Banner,"* but nothing happened. People were frantically turning their heads trying to see the President. Finally, a large, dark-green helicopter landed on the side of the Statue, and the President briskly walked to the podium.

> *"My fellow Americans, I'm very proud to be the first to address you with those words—my fellow Americans, welcome to your country. Of all the things that a President does, nothing is as rewarding as events such as this. This is a ceremony of renewal. With you, today the American dream is reborn…. to always remain 'one nation under God, indivisible, with liberty and justice for all.' Today you've joined a people who are among the freest on the face of the Earth. We're a nation greatly blessed."* **1**

---

[1] **Ronald Reagan** — Excerpts from "Remarks at Naturalization Ceremonies for New United States Citizens in Detroit, Michigan." October 1, 1984.

I couldn't have said it any better. The President invited people to stand up and follow him in reciting the "Pledge of Allegiance." Then, he stood aside and gave the stage to a singer. The guy was as tall as the President, but had long dark hair, and was wrapped in a jumpsuit adorned with sparkling Stars and Stripes. He reminded me of Elvis in his better days, but without the shades. The man didn't seem to be on drugs either. *"Coming to America,"* [2] amplified by the loudspeakers, filled the entire island, and probably was heard across the harbor in downtown Manhattan.

With the song's words ringing in my head, I made my way back to Connecticut. Nana Rachel met the arrival of the new citizen with the entire arsenal of her weaponry laid out on display. We celebrated that special occasion by a lot of gunfire at the range. It took us an hour to get through the shooting of every gun. We had used two large cases of ammunition, a small battery of glass bottles and a few unfortunate squirrels caught in the gunfire. Professor Golubov sat on the side, shaking her head in disapproval. She couldn't wait for us to finish having fun and get back to the porch to have some Sherry.

*****

I walked outside *"Aeroporto Leonardo da Vinci"* in Rome. The very same sliding doors that five years ago let me and my two sorry suitcases into the New World closed behind with a loud whoosh. Back then, I had no home, I had no country, I had no one on this side of the Iron Curtain. I even didn't have any document, except for a small piece of paper called the Exit Visa from the Soviet Union and the word *"stateless"* stamped

---

[2] **"America." Neil Diamond's** song written and originally released in 1980.

in red across its face page. Oh yes, I forgot the eighty US dollars burning my pocket. That was the same eighty dollars that the Russian government had the audacity to give me in exchange for a hundred Rubles of their money worth less than the paper it was printed on. Ironically, that insane exchange worked to my advantage. I was a new man now. The biggest treasure I had was tucked in my shirt pocket. It was a thin, dark-blue booklet with the letters embossed in gold *"United States of America."*

I had an entire day before catching my overnight train to Milan. Five years ago, I had spent six weeks here waiting for the entrance visa to the United States. Back then, I had seen some of the Eternal City, but I couldn't taste it on a meager stipend immigration assistance organization had provided. What could one go see, if one would have a day in Rome, and could afford a little splurging to do? To help me with this difficult choice was the exchange rate between US dollar and Italian Lira. In a matter of a few minutes after stepping on the Italian soil, I had discovered another amazing capitalist trick. At that time, for every US dollar, I was getting two times as much in Italian currency. It was like buying everything at half-price. What was even more amazing, I would be paid for my work in the US dollars and make twice as much as my peer-Italian-engineers. I certainly could buy in Italy twice as much as back in the US.

Deep in these thoughts, I found myself standing in front of a massive, long and almost black from soot building. Huge red letters on top spelled *"Roma Termini."* It was the Central Railroad Station. I had already checked in my suitcase in a locker room and was ready to go on the town. Dark-green city buses packed side streets around *Termini*, aimlessly idling, emitting black smoke through their roof stacks. No wonder, the entire city was covered in soot.

It was hot in the middle of July in Rome, even early in the morning. The first order of business was to have an Italian breakfast. Back five years ago, I kept wondering about every bar serving a specific fare each morning. The Italians called it *"cappuccino a cornetto."* Following my old Soviet instinct, *"never-eat-anything-at-the-railroad-station,"* I walked a few blocks away. (That instinct may work well in Europe but not anywhere else. Later on, I had discovered that the best eateries in town were around the railway station, like in Kyoto, for instance). Soon, I found out that it wasn't that simple when it came to ordering your coffee in Italy. The Italians could have their morning coffee in a dozen of different ways. When the barman saw my empty look and figured that he had no chance to get out of me how I wanted my coffee, he promptly decided that it needed to be a *"caffè americano."* I didn't like it. It was too much water. To add an insult to the injury, they didn't serve a "bottomless cup of coffee," even they called it American. A good Italian Samaritan came to my rescue seeing me struggling. It turned out that he knew what I liked, and ordered a *"double-shot espresso cappuccino."* The same thing happened with *cornetto*. I hated it. It was a hollow pastry roll, cold as hell. My new Italian friend figured that one too. He ordered a French *croissant*. That little miracle of a buttery and flaky pastry named for its well-known crescent shape had arrived hot. So much for my Italian breakfast — American coffee with a French pastry…

While munching on my croissant, I got educated by my new friend on the intricacies of Italian coffee-making. If the barman pushed on me a *"caffè lungo,"* I wouldn't have liked it either. It would come from the same espresso machine, but with the double amount of water than in usual espresso, unlike *"caffè americano"* diluted with hot water after brewing. In any way, I looked at it, it was still full of water I would be paying for. And that was just a tip of the iceberg of Italian coffee culture.

He was ready to go on when I threw my hands up and quickly declared my future breakfast preferences in Italy. It took me all of four dollars on this experimentation.

The fellow who came to my rescue happened to have his breakfast in that bar every morning before heading to his office at the *"Universita Di Roma - La Sapienza"* [3] When he learned that I had a full day on my hands, he offered to show me what simple mortals usually don't come to Rome see. I suppose that tourists didn't use a way of transportation I was offered, too. It was a scooter parked at the bar's door. Apparently, helmets were not in a high fashion. Sidewalks were considered an undeniable extension of the road. The red traffic light was a matter of opinion, not an order to stop! I put my dear life in the hands of a stranger, and closed my eyes, peeking occasionally from behind his back. We bravely cut across lanes. We weaved our obnoxious way forward, sometimes jumping curbs and riding over sidewalks. I was relieved when we arrived at his office at the University. I unglued my sweaty hands from the leather jacket of my driver, and happily stood on my two feet on the firm ground.

The summer semester was over. The building was empty of students. My new friend's name was Carlo. Carlo was about my age, and close by complexion. His black hair grew disorderly out from any possible place of his head. Parts of his face not covered with hair seemed even smaller behind a large-rimmed simple glasses prominently displayed in front of his eyes. He had big and protruding lips exposing rows of not so straight teeth. But his black beard and mustache were neatly trimmed and fitted his face. His eyes were alive with excitement, and he looked happy. The entire Carlo's appearance reminded me of a student anticipating a new

---

[3] **"La Sapienza — Knowledge."** The university of Rome.

discovery going to happen at any given moment. Carlo was an assistant professor of Roman Archeology and History while finishing his doctorate paper. He spent summertime with his students digging around Rome, or the vast expanse of the former Roman Empire. He assured me that *"what I see above the ground is nothing. Everything, all of the two thousand years of the Roman history is buried under our feet."* I was happy to hear that he had a solid job security for the next two thousand years to unearth all those treasures.

We hopped back on his *"motorino,"* the Italian way of calling scooters, and dived into a labyrinth of the Rome's streets. Those streets had not become any wider since the time they had been built for a horse and buggy. Now I could see a clear benefit of his motorized contraption.

"Here is your embassy," Carlo pointed his hand ahead.

I still couldn't get over that I was an American. I was so proud that the United States was my country now. *"Yep... It was...,"* I recognized the building where five years ago I had gotten my American visa. I barely held back my emotions, maintaining a casual way about it. The street, *Via Veneto* was busy. Carlo crossed in front of oncoming traffic to the other side of the street and casually jumped the curb in front of a fancy hotel. We drove for a while on the sidewalk until he cut into a tiny street and stopped by a church. A small line of tourists crowded a side entrance. He chained his contraption to the cast-iron fence and pulled me inside the church through the main doors. A monk dressed in a plain brown robe with a hood hurried towards us. A simple rope was tied around his waist. He wore leather sandals over bare feet. He greeted Carlo as an old friend and unlocked a small door leading down under the floor.

"Do you wonder why your morning coffee is called cappuccino?" Carlo asked all of a sudden.

It had not occurred to me, yet...

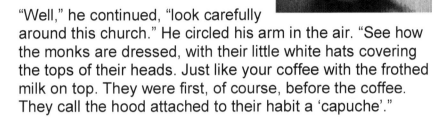

"Well," he continued, "look carefully around this church." He circled his arm in the air. "See how the monks are dressed, with their little white hats covering the tops of their heads. Just like your coffee with the frothed milk on top. They were first, of course, before the coffee. They call the hood attached to their habit a 'capuche'."

He flipped a switch on the wall. A meager light from a yellow bulb shed onto narrow stone steps leading into the darkness ahead. We started going down and soon reached a small landing. It was eighty degrees out on the street, but down there, I started to fill some chill. I could hear a water dripping, running in thin strings down a thick brick wall into a ditch carrying it somewhere further below. The steps continued down, but Carlo suddenly stopped and opened a small wooden door in the wall. We came out into a chamber. I thought that I ended up in a horror movie. The entire walls and ceiling were lined up with human bones and skulls. Mummified corpses dressed in the identical brown robes with the hood sat, stood and lay scattered around. They looked intact as if it was a casual scene of their life snapped and frozen in time.

We slowly walked through five vaulted rooms. Every inch of the walls and ceilings was used to house the remains of the monks.

"Quello Che Voi Siete Noi Eravano. Quello Che Noi Siamo Voi Sarete."

"What you are now, We used to be. What we are now, You will be."

I heard a calm Carlo's voice reciting every man's destiny. He kept quiet for a while before speaking again,

> "I want to show you something tourists don't see. A Capuchin monastery in Brno, *Czechoslovakia* recently donated their dead monks to this church. Somehow, they stayed preserved better than anywhere else. It must be a special air there..."

We went out the same way we came in and continued further down the narrow stone steps to the next landing. Carlo pushed another wooden door in.

Twenty-four monks lay perfectly preserved, arranged in rows across the floor. They were clad in robes, some holding rosaries, or clutching a crucifix. Just a few lay peacefully, but others had fear on their lifeless faces. That was intense to behold. *"What you are now, We used to be. What we are now, You will be."* Carlo's voice sounded in my head. His real voice came through my thoughts,

"They had never intended to create mummies out of themselves. The monks re-used a single coffin time and time again. After the funeral, they would move the deceased into the crypt and lay him to rest on a pillow of bricks. The dry air did the rest, gradually preserving the bodies where they lay. The monks kept placing their deceased under the church floor for three hundred years. At the end of the eighteenth century, that practice was banned. Those monks are pretty aged."

Carlo deeply sighed, and continued,

"We found a few bodies accidentally buried alive. 'The errors' had been common until recently when paralysis and coma were better understood. More than one unfortunate person in the crypt met this fate. See that woman..." He pointed to a well-preserved corpse.

Riding his scooter to *Termini* seemed even scarier than before, after a sober reminder by the Capuchin monks that our passage on Earth is swift, and our own mortality is inevitable. We shook hands. His was a small and soft of a scholar.

*****

6. Milan

End of July in Milan didn't seem any different from July in any large city. The morning rush-hour crowd seemed tired from work and ready for a vacation. I took the "green" subway line, transferred to the "red," and emerged back into the bright sunshine of the blue Milanese sky. A small hotel where I was booked was in a quiet quarter, surrounded by four-storied, old style apartment buildings. For a few weeks, it would be my temporary home, until I found an apartment. I dropped my bag and went to the nearest bar to try out my newly-acquired breakfast skills, and meet with the company's European representative who supposed to be there. He was. It was a stocky man in his forties by the name Frank, or Francisco as he asked to call him in Italy. In the rest of Europe, he didn't mind to be called Frank. He lived in Munich and arrived by overnight train to show me around.

He was duly impressed by my punctuality and by my confident skills of ordering the food, considering that I had only been in Italy for twenty-four hours. We got out of the bar and walked over to a tiny car. I thought that it was a motorcycle with a cabin built around it, and fully expected to find a set of handles attached to the front wheel.

"Those bastards at the rail station didn't have anything else for rent, but this junk," frustrated Francisco threw his arm at someone invisible in the air. "Don't be shy. Please, squeeze yourself in," he opened the door.

I noticed silver letters glued to its grill "*Cinquecento. Fiat 500.*" The size of that tin-can was a half of any small American sedan. The good news was, it was bright yellow and hard to miss. The bad news was, I was sitting so low that my ass seemed to scrape the road. The ride was as scary as my *"motorino"* travels around Rome the day before. But the scariest part was riding along a truck or a city bus. I kept looking up at a relentlessly rotating huge tire near my face, and thinking, *"Hope, the driver is watching the road... Hope, he is not making any turns..."* It sounded like a prayer. I could use a prayer, getting on the road in that contraption called a car. Luckily, we were not going on the highway. The car was almost square and could fit into any hole to park forward, backward, or sideways — it wouldn't really matter. But for all practical purposes of a large city, that car served its purpose.

By ten in the morning, Francisco rolled his contraption into a narrow opening between two large cars in front of an office building. Any normal car wouldn't fit in, of course. I climbed out and straightened my back. Thank G-d for small miracles! We went in and took an elevator up. A glass door on the third floor had golden letters spelling *"Alfonsi Industrial Consultants."* Frank walked in with a casual familiarity and announced to the receptionist that we were to see Mr. Alfonsi himself. Apparently, we were expected, and advised to proceed to his office.

He knocked and entered without an invitation. The man behind the desk slowly lifted his head up. He took off his reading glasses as if trying to recognize the disruptors of his morning peace. A tiny string of steam was still curling up from his coffee. The man got up from his leather chair and walked around the desk. Francisco and this man looked like they were twin-brothers, or at least had one parent in common. I was sure that they used to hear it all the time. Mr. Alfonsi stretched out his small and puffy hand and introduced himself. Then said,

"Well Francisco, please, sit down. And you, young man, too. Is it true?" He looked at me with his small, dark, piercing eyes. Apparently, he realized that I didn't get it, and quickly

63

added, "Is it true? That you are an engineer! That young!"
He didn't wait for my answer and continued staring at me,
"*Signore Dottore,* I have a ton of work for you already. See
that pile on the floor in the corner? These are all technical
manuals. Do you think you can handle that?"

"Enrico! C'mon!" Frank quickly interfered. "You know, the
agreement, I suppose... He just got off the plane. Give him
a break. Besides, did you secure the course for him to
start? He hardly knows two words in Italian."

It seemed that Mr. Alfonsi was surprised, but quickly regained
his control,

"But of course! The young man can start even today. We
have a professóre from the university on retainer. Just say
when, young man...," he looked at me. "That's what I
thought... He needs a little breathing room. I have an idea,
let Nicolá work with this fellow." He stopped and looked at
me again, "Nicolá is my son. He's about your age... Let him
get involved. One day, he would take over the business...,
hopefully. Besides, let them young people work together.
They understand each other better. I'll set up an office for
you here. You can come and go as you please. Agreed?"
He didn't wait for my answer, "Let's go! I would like my son
to meet the new *Dottore.*"

When we walked into Nicolá's office, he was on the phone.
Hurriedly, he sent some *"Ciao-s"* into the receiver, hung up,
and walked around his desk to greet us.

*****

Nicolá didn't look like his dad, at all. He must've taken after
his mother — the better half, I assumed. Nicolá was tall, slim,
dark-haired, and with dark-brown eyes. He must've been
about my age. We hit it off from the first day I came to the

office. He set me up in a small room next to his and made it our hangout place. Once, he learned about my Russian roots, he had his dad's secretary put some pictures of Moscow and Leningrad on the walls, and a few flower pots around the room. I couldn't figure the meaning of the flowers, but it was a nice touch. I hated the pictures, though. I didn't want to hurt Nicolá's feelings, suspecting that he, like a lot of Italians, could've had a special fondness for the Soviet Union. At the end of my first week in the office, I had quietly removed them from the walls. Nicolá noticed but didn't say anything. The next day, he brought some watercolors of Rome. That time, he let me choose the ones to hang up, hoping that I would come to like Rome the way he loved it.

Nicolá became my new buddy. I even moved into his apartment from the hotel, while looking for my own. Nicolá was the only son and the heir apparent of the owner of the largest in Europe consulting enterprise dealing with all sorts of foreign industrial things. Nicolá's father Enrico was a short, stocky and a balding man in his fifties. It appeared that he ruled his fiefdom with an iron fist. The office was large and employed all kinds of different folks. One thing was apparent, though. Whenever Enrico was walking through, a deadly silence was in the air. At all other times, the office was full of phone chatter and buzz. I came to call him jokingly *Don Enrico*, even in his face. He called me *Signore Dottore*, and I thought he was joking, too. He wasn't! He was dead serious! As I quickly learned, the Italians held in a very high esteem someone who was able to reach a high level of education, especially if it was in engineering, especially at my young age. People with such education, regardless of the field, were generally referred to as a *Dottore*.

The first five months of my life in Milan were, to say the least, busy. I had not seen anything but the office, my Italian class at the university, and my bed in Nicolá's apartment. I put every possible effort into conquering another language, attending *"Italian as a second language"* class, or was it a "third language" for me... The whole idea of choosing me for the "Italian job" rested on an American perception that if I knew one European language, the next would come to me by itself..., without any effort, and fast. The Americans thought that all European languages were the same, and with a slight tweak, I would be speaking Italian in a week or two. I tried hard not to disappoint folks back home at the factory.

I realized that it was already Christmas when Josie appeared one day in my office. I didn't see her with my back turned to the door and my feet up on the window sill. I was about to explode. Using my last drops of patience, I was trying to calmly explain to an Italian engineer on the other end of the line how some American contraption worked.

While assisting Frank in selling our industrial gadgets to clients in Western Europe, I quickly discovered that a sale by itself wasn't the end of the process. Just the opposite, it was a beginning of hopefully-long for our factory relationship with a client, leading to many more sales in the future. After a sale was consummated, the equipment would be delivered, unpacked and installed by our factory people. The Italians usually had been trained with my assistance. Supposedly, I already knew the language. Somehow, it worked.

It was one of the not-talked-about tasks which came with my job description. It was another side of the business. Some Italian clients wanted me to keep working with their engineers. They wanted me to "hang around" and keep explaining what we already had explained when we had trained them in the first place. The dirty little secret was that many Italian engineers needed a "hand-holding," as Nicolá put it subtly. What it really meant was that they liked someone around them all the time: while they studied the documentation, used the equipment, and broke it, sometimes by not using it correctly. I only had so many hours in the day.

So Josie stood quietly by the door of my office until I heard Nicolá's excited voice,

> "Why are you keeping this beauty in your door frame? She deserves to be framed with spring flowers…, like…" It didn't take him too long to come up with, "Like…, like the *Botticelli's Primavera.*"

I recited his words in English to my client on the phone. I thought I got the translation right but stopped in the middle of the sentence once I turned my chair around. Josie was the last person I expected to see. She allowed Nicolá kiss her hand and made a curtsy. With her hand still sticking out, she walked straight to my desk,

> "Aren't you joining in?" She said playfully.

Nicolá disappeared. He returned in a few minutes with three tall glasses, a bottle of a sparkling *"Prosecco"* dry wine, and a box of *"Baci,"* chocolates from nearby Perugia.

> *"Buon Natale!... Buon Natale!... Buon Natale a tutti!"*[4]

I finally realized that Christmas had arrived, and with it, my "gift" wrapped in Italian leather. Josie came in this morning and managed to do some shopping in Milan already. According to Nicolá, the only better place than Milan to shop for the Italian leather was Florence.

> "Guess what? I got an assignment for a year in London! It is an hour-hop by plane from here," Josie announced joyfully.

---

[4] **Merry Christmas, Merry Christmas, to everyone!** Ital.

I didn't know what to say, how to react. I stupidly grinned, looking at Nicolá for help. He turned to her and said,

"Why don't we go to Tuscany for Christmas. My dad has a place near Siena. You would like it down there."

The morning of the Christmas Eve, we came down from the apartment just to find that a lovely girl was waiting for us.

"Hey Ragazzi, meet my friend Velia. She is joining us for the trip." Nicolá watched me for reaction.

Velia was a tall, slender, dark-haired girl in her mid-twenties. She had a straight nose, what they called in Italy the Roman profile. Her large blue eyes didn't belong to her strong face, giving it a touch of softness. She had large, sensitive, red lips and white, sparkling teeth. At all times, her mouth was slightly open as if gasping for air like a fish out of the water. According to Nicolá, Velia's family could trace their roots all the way to the Patricians of the Ancient Rome. Her family owned a few apartment buildings in Milan, and had a large estate west from the city, in Piedmont, near the border with France, where they grew grapes for their own wine. Velia arrived at our door in a white two-sitter *Maserati*, and now stood casually leaning on her ride.

"I don't think we can fit into this... We are taking my *'Alfa-Romeo.'* "

Nicolá quickly ran around the corner, and soon appeared in his large car. It was a five-hour drive through the Italian countryside. We stopped a few times at small places to savor local prosciutto, cheese, fresh bread and fruit. Every time, we had a bottle of a red wine with it. By the time we rolled in the yard of the house, we were sufficiently drunk and loud.

"If we still care for dinner, we'd better drive down to Siena. In a couple of hours, everyone will be gone to eat their seven-fish dinner."

The road to town was narrow and winding around the hills with dense woods coming to the edge of the road. We were the only car at that late afternoon hour. *"I shouldn't drink at dinner,"* I thought, *"someone had to get us in the dark back to the house."* Then I remembered,

"Nicolá, what was that 'seven-fish dinner,' you mentioned in the house?"

The girls in the back were trying to discuss Josie's new leather coat and the bag she got yesterday. It was a monumental task considering they didn't speak a common language. Nicolá interfered a few times translating, but quickly gave up. I could see he was concentrating on the road. I wouldn't ask about the 'seven-fish dinner,' if I knew that it wasn't a simple one-sentence answer.

"We call it *'La Vigilia di Natale* or *The Christmas Vigil.'* The Italians are not supposed to eat but fast in anticipation of the Christmas dinner. Funny, the new tradition had come here from America. You guys are the rich of the world who could afford seven dishes in one meal. Since the Christmas dinner has been here forever, we didn't want to replace it. Thanks to you, we have two feasts now. Anyway, the number seven is for the seven sacraments of the Catholic Church. The dishes vary, depending on where you find yourself in Italy, but normally you can expect some anchovies, whiting fish, lobster, sardines, eels, squid, octopus, shrimp, mussels, and clams, and, of course, *Baccalà,* what we call a dried salt cod."

Listening to Nicolá, I didn't notice that we arrived at the main Siena square.

"Can you imagine that twice each summer, they race horses and chariots around this small place," Nicolá commented.

The square was formed as a fan and was laid with the pale-brick pavement.

"Let's take a walk. You'll feel it under your feet, it is not flat. It is like a seashell."

We walked around for a while and got back in the car. A few blocks away, Nicolá parked on the sidewalk near a medieval wall served as a foundation for apartments upstairs. A small family restaurant, *"Osteria,"* was inside the wall at the street level.

"You, guys should try their *'pasta Pici.'* This pasta is a thick spaghetti with sage and almond sauce. If someone craves for more, their specialty is toasted *Polenta* with a cream sauce and spicy Tuscan sausage. Tonight, it's on me. Pig out, Ragazzi!"

We returned to the house with the first stars popping up in the dark-blue sky. It started to get cold in the hills. While the girls stayed in the house unpacking, Nicolá and I went out to get some wood for the fireplace. He startled me with his question,

"Is Josie your girlfriend? Are you guys going seriously?"

Up to that very moment, I had been so busy with everything around me in Italy that I felt that I had left my life in the US far behind. Josie was a big part of it but still left behind for the time being. I wasn't prepared to place her in my life here. A few times, it occurred to me that I should start going partying with Nicolá. But every time, Nicolá asked me to join him, I couldn't get away from my daily avalanche of things. Nicolá was only waiting for me to get into the "groove of the Italian life," the way he put it, before we would start our forays onto the bachelor scene of Milano. Clearly, Josie wasn't included in the plans. Now it seemed like a possibility. It had been a while since I had sex, and it was with Josie. Past night was great. She stayed over, instead of returning to her hotel.

I explained to Nicolá my precarious situation. He thought for a second and said philosophically,

"One does not bring a date to a whore-house." Of course, it sounded more palatable in Italian.

"Well," he continued, "then, in this case, I always wanted to try some American pussy. Perhaps, you have a similar desire towards our Italian ladies…" He looked at me, waiting for an answer.

We walked in the house carrying logs of wood. I went straight to the fireplace to get the fire going. Nicolá was stupidly grinning. Like a lazy cat, he danced his way towards the girls comfortably sitting on the couch and sipping red wine.

"Ladies, you have a privilege of tasting one of the best wines the humanity ever produced," he casually started. "It is a local Chianti. My dad is big on it. If you care for going down into the cellar, you would see lots of Chianti. One thing I can tell you that it is almost impossible to buy a bottle wrapped in a straw basket. We call it a 'fiasco,' but it is not what you may think… It is a flask."

Josie grabbed the bottle and poured
two full glasses for Velia and herself.

"I spent one entire summer down
here learning about growing
grapes and the winemaking. This
classic Chianti consists of three-
quarters of the *Sangiovese grape,*
and the rest is a mix of *Canaiolo,*
and, surprisingly, a white grape, *Malvasia Bianca.* Well, it is
boring, I suppose... Velia, your family owns some
vineyards. Are you still interested in wines?"

She nodded a few times in agreement, and said,

"... But I am interested in something else too. I know what
this wine goes well with...," she looked at Nicolá. "Why don't
you go and bring your magic box."

Nicolá disappeared for a moment and returned holding a
wooden ornamented case.

"I keep my babies in a humidor. Help yourselves, ladies."

They took slim cigarettes from the box and lit them up. A
familiar smell of the dorms at UConn hit my nostrils. The room
went quiet for a while. A blue smoke was curling up from the
couch. I was busy building fire, not paying much attention to
their chatter. Then my ears perked at the next thing Nicolá
said,

"Ladies, my American buddy and I have an offer for you," he
took a long pull on his cigarette. "Well," he hesitated, " what
if we all get naked in front of the fire, and see what
happens..."

Considering that the ladies didn't speak a word of each other language, they had arrived at their decision remarkably quickly,

> "As long as you boys use condoms…," announced Josie. She quickly added, "And something else… No double-dipping and shuttling between us with the same condom. Use a fresh one…"

We gladly accepted the rules. It was dark and cold outside. I could hear the wind playing with the barn door left loose. It kept screeching going back and forth and slamming with a loud noise. A lonely owl was crying in the woods. Inside, the fire was dancing, blasting the heat waves in the room. I went to wash up. When I returned, I found Josie standing on all fours in front of the fireplace. She was completely naked. Velia, also naked, stood behind her on her knees, studying the tattoo on her lower back. In one hand, she had a glass of wine, and in another, the joint. She was discussing the intricacies of the design with Nicolá. I could tell that Josie was enjoying the study of her behind in the melodic language she didn't understand. She stood motionless with a wide smile on her face and with her nipples moving up and down with each breath she took. I stopped by the door and watched, waiting for further developments. Nicolá got off the couch. He was fully aroused, watching the girls. He came to Velia from behind and hugged her kissing her neck. She gently protested, and pointed at Josie. Nicolá turned to me and quickly translated,

> "Velia moved me *'one car'* forward. The way I started would only work if we were gay. You, mister, are going to mind the back of our choo-choo train…"

With those very words, he moved into Josie from behind, and waved at me, inviting to get into Velia. We crawled around a small circle at a slow pace, sounding silly train sounds, but fully joined. The last stop was in front of the fire. We refilled our tanks with wine, took more pulls on our joints, and happily came, almost altogether.

"We call it 'The American train' here. Do you know what a European choo-choo train is, Ragazzi?" said Velia sprawled on the rug and looking at the ceiling. Her large, purple nipples perked.

"Oh, dear! No! Velia! Please, you don't want to go there," begged Nicolá. But after a short discussion in Italian, he agreed to explain,

"A guy, or could be a girl for that matter, blows weed smoke into a girl's asshole. The girl clenches it tight while they are having sex. She orgasms and the weed smoke blasts out."

I was laughing so hard that developed hiccups. To stop it, I took a big gulp of Chianti, but couldn't hold it. I burst it all out, probably like that orgasmic girl would blast the smoke out of her ass. A thousand of little red droplets splattered naked bodies of Velia and Josie and the floor around them. Suddenly, Velia got serious, sat straight and said,

"You know, Ragazzi, I would love to have a tattoo like Josie's, but with my own twist. My name means 'concealed' in Italian. "

She took another pull on her cigarette, following with a gulp of wine. Josie moved on the floor rug, turned on her side and started intently listen to Nicolá translating,

"You guys heard of the Sistine Chapel in Rome, of course. Michelangelo had spent four years hanging under the ceiling and painting the frescoes. They think that he had buried symbols of the female anatomy in the paintings.

74

The most obvious are eight ram skulls, which positioned at regular points around the ceiling. They separate the nude male and female pairs. I'll show it to you."

Velia ran out of the room and returned with her handbag. After a short struggle searching through its bowels, she put a piece of paper on the table. We all leaned over it. There was some resemblance... *"One can liken the uterus to anything, depending on how far the imagination could fly. Beauty is in the eye of the beholder, as they say, "* I thought, but didn't say anything.

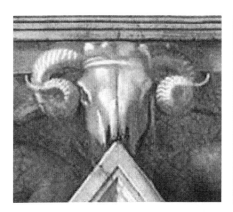 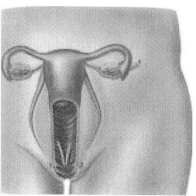

"There are other things hidden in the frescoes. I am thinking to get a tattoo with something meaningful to be concealed in it. Josie's is great! Perhaps, I might use it and hide a small vagina in it. I might just do vagina on its own merit."

"I think vagina certainly deserves it. Every man comes out of there, then all his life, trying hard to get back," said Josie, finally fully awake.

It was a timely observation. I was looking at two gorgeous vaginas right in front of my eyes, but what a difference it was. Unlike Josie's cleanly waxed with just a thin vertical sliver of hair left in the middle, Velia's was hidden behind an expansive charcoal bush. The matching growth was under her armpits. I suppose it was a European thing. I remembered that back in the Soviet Union, girls, at least the ones I had known, wore the same style.

With all that talk about vaginas, I couldn't concentrate on the paper for too long, constantly diverting my attention to the beauties I could touch. We quickly put off Velia's tattoo struggle till the next morning and moved back to the fireplace rug to ride our choo-choo train.

It snowed the next morning. The surrounding hills turned white, and the road became icy. We decided to spend that Christmas day in. Luckily, the cellar was stocked with wine and cheese. Nicolá brought along an endless supply of condoms and weed. We could stay there until the next spring.

*****

7. The Russian Connection

We returned to Milan three days after Christmas. Velia went straight to a tattoo parlor. That same evening, we celebrated the new addition to Velia's body in the hotel where Josie stayed. The American taxpayer, through the State Department where Josie was employed, picked up the tab. It was a nice touch to allow Josie to come to Europe a few days before her job started in London. She had to visit a dying aunt in Milan, of course. It was a white lie, but it was for a good cause. Velia's back was sore, but it didn't stop her from having sex in a more conventional way. We had to be gentle with her, though. Josie stayed till the New Years. Early morning of January first, she took a train back to London.

One day in late January, Nicolá's father, Mr. Alfonsi himself, appeared in my office door. He gently pushed in another gentleman, introducing him as Evgeny from Russia.

"We are opening an office in Moscow. Comrade Eugine, as you Americans say, will work with us in Milan to make sure everything running smoothly," joyfully announced Mr. Alfonsi. "The Russians like our Italian cars. They are negotiating to modernize an old factory that had been built by one of our automakers many years ago. It looks like it may happen soon."

Mr. Alfonsi went to the door and closed it tightly.

"Now," he looked conspiratorial, "this is only between us! Capisce?"

He paused for a while to give more importance to the moment, and continued,

"I know that you have a contract for a year with your employer from back home. I know that you have to do your job. What I am asking you to do is to take a look at an offer I have prepared. I will understand if you say *'Net'* to it. No hard feelings! Sleep on it, young fellow."

He shook my hand, patted me on the shoulder, and left with his guest in tow, leaving a thin leather folder on my desk. The last few weeks after the New Year was busy with work, but I still had some free time. I finished my crash course in Italian at the university and started getting a hang of the language, at least, for my work communications. I sat down and opened the folder. When I finished reading, it was dark outside. Nicolá barged in, holding two glasses and a bottle of white wine.

"I know that you don't like white, but you must try this *'Bordeaux'*!"

"I don't drink white piss, you know it!" I resisted slightly, but took a sip.

"Look, fellow, I wouldn't give you a piss. By now, you should know better than to question my taste in wines. I remember you resisted Chianti in my house in Siena hills too… Then, someone couldn't have enough of it. Of course, the weed made it even better, perhaps."

Nicolá didn't have to persuade me. I emptied the glass, slowly sipping it, and asked for more. It was dry and had a light taste of lime, vanilla, lemon, and nuts. Any of these flavors could easily kill the wine, but they were mixed in that bottle to perfection. I could only feel a slight hint of them. The wine was silky and smooth. Nicolá was silently watching me.

"I took interest in winemaking when dated Velia." I noticed he used the past tense. "Her family has vineyards in France, too. One summer, we had spent a few weeks in

Pessac-Léognan, just south of the city of Bordeaux. It is so close to the city that some of the vineyards are completely surrounded by the housing areas. A good white Bordeaux is a mix of just two grapes: *Semillon* and *Sauvignon Blanc*. When they start to add to that mix something else, don't waste your money... The same is with the red Bordeaux, by the way. *Cabernet Sauvignon* and *Merlot* are the two magic grapes to make a great red Bordeaux. We, the Romans, taught them French bastards the winemaking in the first century." Nicolá finished proudly.

For a while, we sat silently. Nicolá spilled evenly the remaining wine.

"Did my dad mention anything about this Russian guy Evgeny?"

I nodded, but didn't say anything. Nicolá shifted in his chair, and said,

"If the business with the Russians will really take off, my dad wants to be on the ground floor. Right under us," Nicolá stomped on the carpet, "one floor below, we have a department that does translations of technical manuals for some clients. They use German, French, and some English language. We do not have anyone with the Russian. He will pay you anything you ask if we get this business."

Reading his father's offer, I got a good idea of what he wanted to do. Once the Russians cleared the way for the Italians to rebuild a car factory, a ton of technical stuff had to be translated into Russian. Mr. Alfonsi offered me to get together with him on the ground floor. I would start small, just with a secretary, and perhaps, find another translator. Once the business started to grow, I could run an entire operation. He could let me hire as many people as I would need.

The offer was one of those that was hard to refuse. But...
I had some huge reservations. First, I had to finish my
contract. I certainly didn't have any plans to settle down in
Europe. I knew for sure that in a year or two, I wanted to go
back to my country, the United States, where I belonged.
Second, but as important, I hated the Soviet Union, and to
help them was against my religion, as they say in America.
I suspected that some good money could be made, but at
what price to me?

I slept on it for a week, feeling quite uncomfortable. No one
bothered me with the answer. Finally, I went to see Mr.
Alfonsi. My rationale was simple. I felt that while I was in
Milan, I could get a better picture where that business could
go. I was poor as a church mouse (another pearl from my
notebook Mr. Wieber gave me). I wouldn't mind making some
money before I return to the States, considering that living in
Italy was very cheap on the American dollar I had been paid
with.

Mr. Alfonsi got excited. We sat in his office burning midnight
oil till no one else remained in the entire building. He
expected the contract between the Russians and the Italians
to be signed in the spring, and preliminary documentation
would be needed by the midsummer. My contract should end
at that same time, leaving me with a decision to be made.
Meanwhile, Mr. Alfonsi would set up a new office for me on
the floor below.

They bought me the most modern Russian typewriter, and put
an ad in a newspaper for a Russian speaking secretary,
hoping to find one to do my typing. Every day, I spent an hour
or two typing translations with one finger. Nicolá liked to stop
by my offices (I had two now). He thought that he was helping
me with getting through a boring day. I wasn't bored at all, but
it felt relaxing to break away and bullshit with him for a while.

Just like he did with my first office, Nicolá took in his hands the decoration of the second one. He had learned his lesson the first time and put on my walls the watercolors of Rome. With some cautious glances towards me, he added two pictures of Siena. I could figure his reasoning behind the Siena's pictures, but more of Rome, again…? Apparently, he had a good reason. His own office ran out of walls. One day, when I was particularly busy, Nicolá decided to enlighten me on his family history. His mother was a native of Rome. He could talk about the Eternal City for hours — the time I exactly didn't have.

"You know, if not for my dad, I would live in Rome."

Nicolá sat on the corner of my desk, like my boss used to do back home. A very bad habit. He kept talking,

"Rome is a laid-back city. Life in Rome is slow-paced, and to an outsider seems disorderly. The main rule down there is *'if we don't get to it today, we may get to it tomorrow, or the next day, or perhaps, the day after.'* The warm climate plays a role in it. Rome is the city of government bureaucrats, usually not used to working hard, to begin with. Long siestas could often extend to the next morning, and nobody really cares. If you miss someone in the office before noon, don't bother to come back that day again. Come tomorrow! Sometimes, I wonder if the laws of physics work in Rome? Not in the summertime, anyway."

What I had learned already about Milan was directly opposite of Rome, or at least, of a picture, Nicolá painted for me. Milan lived by its own clock, and so did all the Italian North, where most of the industries were situated. Proximity to the rest of Europe put its mark on Milan. A few Germans who came for business to the office had a running joke: *"Anything south of*

Florence is Africa!" The motherf*ckers didn't hold Italy in high regard, and mostly looked at it as just their vacation land to get their fat asses away from the cold.

Regardless of their opinion, the northern Italy was indeed different from the rest of the country. That put a lot of pressure on the Italians who lived there, and especially in Milan. I could tell how difficult it was for the older generation adapting to the "new Europe," moving in the fast lane and trying to catch up with America. For the young folks, it was no problem. The young generation up north didn't have the old, slow Italian mentality. They wanted to be just like their peers in Western Europe. *"We want to live today, we want it all now! Even, if we have to work hard for it."* Many did.

As for me, it was an easy transition. I had never stopped working, except for a brief sojourn in Italy waiting for my immigration visa to enter the United States. Although Nicolá tried hard to ease me into the old-school of Italian work habits, I couldn't do it for a simple reason of juggling my engineering job, the Italian language school, and the recently-added gig for his dad, Mr. Alfonsi.

On one of those "dull" days, I was busy typing a document of some turbine made by a German company for an electric plant somewhere in Russia. (Just imagine, not that long ago, the Germans had trashed the country to the ground and now busy rebuilding it). Nicolá quietly opened my door and invited himself in. For a while, he kept silent, watching. When he saw me stopping for a second, he immediately intervened,

"What if you teach me Russian. It seems that our business is growing in that direction. One day, I may need to travel over there. It would be nice to know a couple of words here and there…, pick up some Russian blonds in Moscow… What would you say?"

I lifted my head up from the papers, and stared at him for a few moments,

"I tell you what…," I started. "I'd be delighted! But I have a request of my own." Nicolá was all attention now. "I wouldn't mind getting more practice in Italian myself. I mean, in everyday language, but not the street one, more sophisticated Italian, the one, educated people speak. Capisce?"

"No problem. We can start any time your little heart desires!"

We shook hands on it.

*****

I heard a timid knocking on my door. I was working one late evening in my other, *"The Russian office,"* as Nicolá had christened it. The door moved slowly in, and a familiar face showed up in the opening.

"May I?" Evgeny shyly asked in Russian.

I waved him in. He started a small talk, but I asked him to cut to the chase.

"As you wish, comrade."

Apparently, after mentioning that *"comrade,"* my face turned blue. I didn't leave the Soviet Union to still remain someone's comrade. I was about to get up, and, under some silly excuse, ask him politely to leave. Sensing it, he rushed to speak,

"You know, we can be very good friends. I have many connections here in Milan. You can make a lot of money if we play our cards right."

"We? As in 'You and I?' " He ignored my question, but continued,

"Well, we would need some other people to get involved, too. Of course, Mr. Alfonsi and his son, your friend, have to be a part of it, but there is someone else I'd like you to consider bringing in…"

"I have no clue what you are talking about, but I feel that I am going to pass on your generous offer."

I got up and started walking towards the door, hoping that Evgeny got the hint. He didn't, and kept sitting in the chair by my desk. It took him another invitation to get finally out. Just before closing the door behind himself, he said,

"You might regret that you didn't take my offer. Sleep on it."

I quickly forgot about that conversation, until three weeks later, I found myself visiting Josie in London. It was Easter time, and most businesses in Italy shut down for a few days. Josie kept inviting me to come to London. She settled into her work schedule, found a small apartment in Basewater, and started enjoying her life there.

I took an overnight train to Paris and arrived there very early in the morning. It was an easy switch to an express running under the English Channel. After fourteen hours of travel by train and subway, I emerged out of the London tube in the middle of a quiet residential neighborhood. A large park across the Basewater road spread out as far as my eye could see. A street sign *"Hyde Park"* pointed in that direction. It was a brisk spring day, but a young crowd started setting a picnic on the grass. I walked for a few blocks away from the park and found the right address in a row of townhouses. It was mid-morning, but Josie was still in bed. Her excuse was that I would be pleased to find her there waiting for me. I was pleased. We spent another two hours in bed. The afternoon turned out even better. The weak London sun decided to present the foggy capital with an Easter gift, spilling unusual warmth on its citizens. Josie already learned that one could not waste any time to catch some sun in London. We quickly ran to the nearby market and got a basket full of food, and put our own picnic on the park's grass.

"I am glad you could come. I can show you around tomorrow."

The best thing to do was to get on the "hop-on-hop-off" double-decker and ride two large loops around London on a single ticket. We got off a few times, where Josie thought were important things to see. It seemed to me everything was important. Apparently, some things were more important than others. I didn't argue. I thought the Cornish pasties sold by a tiny shop in the Covent Garden market were the best thing.

Those small pies filled with minced beef and potato were the most delicious food I had eaten in London. There were many other delicious moments, I had that visit, except for one. Josie offered to take me to her office to show around. On the surface, it seemed quite innocent.

She worked for the State Department and her office was inside of the US Embassy compound. It occurred to me that with bringing me to her job, she wanted to put pressure on me about our future together… I still wasn't ready to tie the knot yet.

The US Embassy occupied an eyesore of a building in Mayfair, the fanciest part of London. A spit away from the Buckingham Palace, the five–storied, gray rectangular box stood out by its concrete simplicity. A few green trees couldn't hide the lack of its architectural style. Josie led me through the side entrance for the employees. The front door was reserved for the dignitaries, and some occasional stand-ups the Marines had to hold against crazy demonstrators threatening the sovereignty of our country. Her offices were buried somewhere in the bowels of the building on the third floor. We needed another clearance to step inside very simple quarters. It seemed odd. There was nothing to see. Even early in the morning, people were bored already, lazily chatting after a long weekend. We had some strong coffee, and I was about to bid my farewell when Josie asked me to meet with someone special, the way she put it.

We walked to the end of a long corridor. Josie handed me over to a male secretary in front of a large office and retreated to her end of the building. A tall man with blond receding hair came to greet me. He offered more coffee and showed me to his room. After a small talk about their luck with the good weather in the past weekend, and how fortunate I was to enjoy it all the time in Italy, he asked, all of a sudden,

"Has Mr. Koblukov approached you with anything?"

I had no idea who that "mister" was, and sat, staring at the man with probably a silly look on my face.

"Yes, yes, pardon me," the blond man hurried to add, "Evgeny Koblukov. Has he ever talked to you about anything?"

I told about that strange offer he had made three weeks ago. The man stared quietly at me, then said,

"I am pretty sure you heard about the KGB...," he kept staring at me, probably expecting some reaction. I nodded. "Well," he took a deep breath, "you have two ways to go about it. It seems you have already decided what to do, by telling him off. He is still expecting you to reconsider his offer, though. You can say 'NET,' again, and walk away. Or... You can take his offer. In that case, you wouldn't want to go it alone."

Anybody in the Soviet Union knew very well what the three terrifying letters the blond man mentioned meant. It brought back in my memory the last day in Moscow. I had finished collecting transit visas from different embassies of the countries in Europe, I had to cross. The Austrian embassy was my last stop. Vienna was my final place to reach before I would be met by the people assisting the Soviet refugees on their way to the United States. After obtaining the Austrian visa, I had nothing to do for the rest of the day. I was not too far away from the Red Square. Aimlessly, I wandered towards it.

Somewhere on the way, I turned into a street with a long, gray and cold building. The building was of enormous proportions and spread for the entire block. I walked slowly towards its front. Once at the corner, I looked up and saw

Lubyanka, the name of that street. That made me stop in my tracks in cold sweat. One would have a hard time finding a living soul in Russia who didn't know that blood-chilling name — *The Lubyanka Prison.* I ran into the notorious KGB headquarters. I had never been to that block before. I stopped and spat on the building. It was a purely symbolic gesture, nothing more. If it was for me, I would've leveled it to the ground and planted a park there. It wouldn't be enough room for each and every tree to be planted in that park for every innocent, poor soul perished inside of those walls.

I had to be careful not to attract unnecessary attention. I looked at two guards standing by the front door. Poor bastards, chances were someone in their families had been killed by the very people they were guarding. There was not a single family in the country of a three hundred million people, that had not been affected by the monsters working inside. I spat again at the gray wall and turned away. I never looked back.

The blond man was right, *"I certainly wouldn't want to go it alone. I didn't want to go it at all!"* I sat silently until the man across from me started shifting in his chair.

"You said that there are two ways to deal with Evgeny Koblukov. There is a third way," I said. The man looked puzzled. I continued, "I know someone who is working with him already. You can pitch your offer to him. Thank you for your confidence in me, but I am done with them for good! I am certainly out!"

I got up and shook his hand. On the train back to Milan, I had come to a conclusion that Josie was not meant to be in my life.

*****

8. A Lesson In Italian

The spring was in Milan's air. The weather started getting warmer, even up here in the north. It was Friday morning at the office, and Nicolá already appeared in my door to make plans for the weekend. He never lacked his somewhat crazy plans. I just returned from London and put behind any doubts about my future relation with Josie. It was over. My new plans included starting to get on Milan's singles market. There was one small problem, though. I had to improve my language skills. I reminded Nicolá our conversation about teaching him Russian, in exchange for improving my Italian. He didn't let me finish. He grinned so wide that I thought he could hurt his face,

"We will start immediately…, this evening, after work!"

We walked out of the building to a small *Trattoria* around the corner. What Italian dinner goes without wine! Following a good tradition, we loaded up on freshly-made *fettuccine alla carbonara* complemented by a healthy dose of the house red. Then heavy from food, but happy, we headed to a place where Nicolá promised to begin my first lesson in classic Italian.

The sun was almost down, and the early twilight blanketed the city. We took Nicolá's small convertible Fiat with its top down through the streets filled with the eerie orange light. I recognized the way he was heading. We drove towards the city's center, in the direction of Milan's large cathedral, *Duomo de Milano. "Great! We're going to discuss gothic architecture tonight. Not bad for the first lesson!"* So I thought.

Soon, the *Great Duomo* was left behind. I barely had enough time to make out gargoyles hiding in the darkness on its roof. Then, I recognized a small square, Nicolá drove us through. There on the monastery wall was the famous *Leonardo da Vinci*'s painting *"The Last Supper." "Not bad for the first lesson! Nicolá has a good taste...,"* went through my head.

We zoomed through the dark square, just as fast as we passed by the Milan's cathedral. Nicolá dived into a labyrinth of tiny streets, where I lost a count of his turns. At last, he stopped the car in front of a two-story villa in a small, scantily lit street. He jumped up the stairs leading to a solid wooden door. Then he waved me from the top, inviting to join him.

"Is this the place? I mean, for our lesson?"

"Yep! This is the place, alright!" He rang a brass bell.

The heavy door opened, and a man dressed in black tuxedo led us in. Quiet classic music played somewhere in the back. The man opened tall double doors and invited us to enter a large room, heavily decorated with oriental rugs. The lights were dimmed. At first, I couldn't see the entire space.

"C'mon, dear! C'mon, come in, Nicolá, dear!" A happy voice sounded from the far corner.

Behind that voice, a small woman appeared from the shadows. She was dressed in a funny and strange manner, to say the least. She reminded me of a last century's countess, who lived in a castle with the count Dracula, perhaps! She had on a heavy-fabric, dark-red, medieval type dress decorated with white ornaments all the way to the floor. The material could perfectly fit for her window curtains... The dress belonged to a museum. I haven't seen anything like that to be worn. The woman had a dark-hair wig and was heavily made up. Her long neck was adorned with two strings of large pearls. She was probably in her seventies.

"Nicolá, darling! How nice of you to visit us tonight! Is this your friend you were raving about...? I was dying to meet him..."

She stuck her tiny hand out. Almost every finger was embraced by a ring. At that very moment, a dozen of young ladies entered the room. The ladies quietly settled themselves down onto couches scattered around. A good half of them were Asian. Nicolá looked at me, grinning. The lights became brighter — someone must've turned the switch up. Now in the light, the older woman didn't seem as the Dracula's wife anymore. She rather looked a Marie Antoinette-sque type, except with the dark hair. While I was busy studying our hostess, Nicolá approached the couch. He bent his head down and took the hand of one of the ladies there. He lifted it up to his lips and kissed. The girl got up. Still holding her hand in his, she followed him behind to the stairway upstairs. Passing me, Nicolá leaned forward and whispered in my ear, *"Don't be shy... It's on me!"* He grinned once again, showing his white teeth, and disappeared upstairs with the girl in tow.

I was stunned. I didn't know what to do. In all my travels, I had never been to an establishment of that nature. One thing was hearing about them, the other — just walking into it, unexpectedly, and without any warning. I sat motionless for a while, contemplating my next move when I heard a small voice of our hostess coming from the corner,

"Come, come, dear... Sit down over here, please."

She pointed to an armchair next to hers. All of a sudden, it reminded me of my visits to my Grandma Dora back in Russia. I vividly remembered her sunlit apartment and the armchair I sat near her. I drifted away, remembering our conversations and the warmth I felt every time I saw her. I deeply sighed… What kind of a strange joke was my mind playing on me?

"Don't you like any of the young ladies here?"

I heard her voice coming through. At that moment, I finally realized I had to do something. *That Nicolá, I'm going to kill him! Sneaky bastard!"* I thought, but heard myself saying something else,

"Of course, of course, they are all lovely girls…, and pretty, too…"
"So what is that stopping you? Go on… Invite one of them upstairs…"

I didn't move. A few more minutes passed in complete silence. I swear I could hear my heart pounding inside. Then I saw the woman waving her hand. The ladies got up and disappeared behind the door, walking out in perfect line formation the same way the walked in before.

"Too bad! Nicolá will be disappointed… Anyway, you know I came from Russia, too…" She turned her small torso towards me, and continued, "I was a teenager when the Russian Revolution had happened."

She rolled her eyes up to the ceiling as if trying to remember those days.

"Would you indulge me in a small favor, young man? I don't have many lucky occasions like this to hear Russian spoken."

That night was full of surprises. What happened next was not her listening to me speaking Russian, but rather it was she who talked all the way. Perhaps, it was her idea of listening to her native tongue. I didn't have much of a choice — either listen to her or go upstairs with a girl.

"My father was a highly-positioned bureaucrat in the Tsarist government. With the first unrests started in January of 1917, he knew we had to get out of the country. He was right. What followed was the end of our world we had lived in. My father also knew that to get to a safe haven, preferably France, we had to cross the World-War-torn Europe. I was the oldest of three sisters. One man and four girls — we had no chance! Many of our friends went south to Odessa, the port on the Black Sea. They hoped to make the crossing to Istanbul, and then, God willing, find their way to France. We heard horror stories of sunken ships and people drowned. Not to mention, we had to get down to Odessa first, through the unrest of the vast Russian land.

My father was a smart and a shrewd man. He took us in a different direction. We headed away from unrests and the war. It was a much longer way to escape, but it was a safe way. We went to Vladivostok, the Russian port on the Sea of Japan. We had traveled six thousand miles east, across the entire country, just to find that there were no boats to take us to Shanghai. That was my father's grand plan. He knew that once we made to Shanghai, he could find a way to bring us to France.

Through his position in the government, he knew that in the past twenty years, Russia had been building the Trans-Siberian Railroad. We had traveled most of it already on the way down to Vladivostok. Papa, that was how we called father, knew that they recently added a new branch, the Trans-Manchurian spur. It crossed northern China and passed through a Chinese town of Harbin. We were at the end of the world already, with nowhere to go. We had no choice but to make our trek back west.

93

Once again, we faced a three-hundred-mile journey through the deserted and frozen land. First, it was along the Chinese border, and then it crossed into Inner Manchuria. For the most of the journey, the temperature outside was -25°C (-13°F) below.

Finally, we had arrived in a frigid boomtown of Harbin in the northeastern China. We were lucky we had survived the journey, but we found ourselves in the middle of a strange town in the strange land. Unlike most other Chinese cities, Harbin had been built recently. It was a small, sleepy fishing village on a riverbank until the Russians had run the railroad shortcut through it on the way to the port-city of Vladivostok. Then the Russians built the town to house workers building the railroad. Many stayed behind and settled down even after the railroad had been completed. In the years before, many Jews from the European parts of the Russian Empire had escaped the pogroms to this area. Later, many thousands of Jews kept coming and settling down there.

Papa wasn't the only one who had that idea to escape the Revolution through China. In the course of the three months that we had stayed in Harbin, hundreds of people had been coming daily from Russia looking to escape. Luckily, Papa saved some money. We could stay quite comfortably in one of a few hotels in town until it was warm enough to make our way to the coast again. This time, it was the Chinese coastal port of *Yingkou*. There, we finally boarded a ship and sailed down to Shanghai. It took us a long six months to arrive at the first stop of our journey on the way to France."

At that moment, Nicolá came down, wearing a stupid grin on his face. He was shaking his head while looking at me. He spread his arms wide open, clearly not understanding why I was still sitting down there. I put my finger to my lips, silencing him down, and pointed to a seat next to mine. Then, I leaned over and whispered in his ear,

"Consider this your first lesson in Russian… Capisce?"

He had no idea what I was talking about but obeyed. Meanwhile, our hostess called out, and the man dressed in black tails, the one who led us in, quietly approached and leaned to her. She whispered in his ear, and he slowly retreated back behind double doors. Everything was quiet and seemed subdued in this place.

"Shanghai! Oh, Shanghai! How I loved and hated it at the same time!"

She sighed, and rolled her eyes to the ceiling,

"Shanghai was a cosmopolitan town even then. It attracted many refugees from all ends of the world. It was a free-port and required no visa or work permit to enter. When we first arrived, we found a very small Russian community there. A huge influx of the Russian people took place just a few months later. The Russian October Revolution of 1917 had blazed up.

Thanks to education, our Papa had provided us back home, we had no problem fitting into the "society." My sisters, mother, and I spoke French and German, and a bit of English. That helped with finding work. We needed it. Papa started running out of money. I found work teaching some wealthy Chinese families French and music. So did my mother. My sisters were still too young to work and continued to be homeschooled by the mother. Papa tried looking for a job, too, but the best he could find was some work at small stores as a counter clerk. Money was hard to come by, and we had to give up on a lot of good things we were used to in St. Petersburg.

The teaching job, although it was steady, was barely enough to support us all. By a sheer accident, I was offered a job as a shop assistant in a dressmaking store in the French Concession — The Shanghai's French Quarter. Once again, I had to thank Papa who pushed me hard back home in Russia to learn French. It was a large fashionable store closely following the latest '*Moda*' or fashion of Paris. The Europeans who lived in Shanghai and the Chinese high society frequented the store. I became friendly with another girl working there. She was English, and a bit older than I was.

Once, she asked me if I would like to earn some money on the side. What do you think my answer was...? So on a Friday night, she took me to a dance hall not far away from the store. As it turned out, she was moonlighting as a taxi-dancer there. A taxi-dancer was a paid partner provided by the dance hall for men looking to learn dancing. The hall guests hired the taxi-dancers on a dance-by-dance basis. Just as with a taxi-cab, a dancer's pay depended on the time she spent on the floor with a client. Believe it or not, I saved my very first silver dollar I had earned in that dance hall..."

She got up and walked to the fireplace. There on the mantelpiece, she opened a small, ornamented wooden box and took out a silver coin.

"Here, take a look. This is my first 'dancing dollar'."

She handed it to me. I looked at Nicolá; he started dozing off. It looked like she was determined to get through her story to the end. At that moment, the butler opened the double doors and rolled in a serving cart. The Russian samovar with a set of heavy glasses in silver holders was neatly arranged on it. Suddenly, Nicolá came back to life,

"Ah… Finally! I love your Russian chai. I love it!"

We were served tea in warm glasses and offered some biscuits. Meanwhile, our hostess continued,

"I was a good dancer. Back in St. Petersburg, Mama took me to a ballet school for a few years. But in Shanghai, it was a different kind of dancing — dances popular in Paris in those days. The old favorites like waltz and foxtrot started to be pushed out by tango and Charleston. I had no problem picking it up, and soon became a 'partner-in-demand.' Men started 'pre-ordering' me for their sessions. They started making some other advances, too. Apparently, the girlfriend of mine was working both angles on the dancing floor. Once, she inquired if I knew that I could make much more money if I would only consider requests going just a little beyond dancing. Tell you the truth boys, by the time the first year rolled by, I had plenty of those 'requests' every night.

With the Russian Civil War in full swing, thousands of exiles flooded into the Shanghai's Russian community. Many Harbin Russians, attracted by Shanghai's booming economy, had moved from Manchuria to the coast, too. At the same time, established Russian communities in Paris and Berlin started barring the recent Russian exiles. They didn't want to mix up with their poor brethren. A large number of them headed east, to Shanghai. Thanks to Papa's early start, we were comfortably settled in our new homeland and didn't have to worry about expensive housing. I managed to set up my two younger sisters with jobs in large stores in the French Concession. That was the center of everything happening in Shanghai. By that time, I decided to leave my store job and start my own dance hall.

You can only imagine that my parents badly wanted to marry me. Countless 'crown-princes', 'counts' and other former 'royalty' kept popping up within the Russian exile communities. They were all claiming a relation to the deposed Russian Tsar and were looking to cash in on that fame. Shanghai wasn't any different. Every time, a new 'prince' showed up, my mother was going out of her way to get me to meet him. Papa took a business approach to the marriage of his daughters. He simply wanted to see an applicant's bank account first. Papa didn't care much for a title. Although, if it came with a fat bank account, he wouldn't mind either.

I didn't care for any of that. I let them play their games, as long as they stayed out of my way. My taxi-dancing gig kept bringing me a comfortable income. I managed to support my family and had saved some. Together with my English friend, we opened our own dance hall. I was twenty years old. At that time in Shanghai, it was unheard of for a woman to own a business. So we had to get a man involved. It was mostly for the cover up, and to have bodyguards, of course. It had to be also a Chinese man. For that privilege, we had to pay to our shadow partner Mr. Wong ten percent of our earnings. In one year, our dance hall had become so popular that we had to turn people away. Our China-man, Mr. Wong, finally started to earn his keep. He had hired a small army of guards to protect our standing in the community. Our club, as we preferred to refer to it, was frequented by most diplomats stationed in Shanghai. Sooner or later, all Western transplants had found their way to our door. Many powerful Chinese men were counted among our patrons, too.

At that point, we had turned the corner. Slowly, we had morphed into a 'one-night-stand-arranging service.' It happened naturally. Some of the patrons asked to hook them up with our taxi-dancer girls; some asked to hook them up with other patrons of the same sex. We didn't discriminate, of course. At that time, women didn't look for our services yet. I started keeping 'The Book of Appointments,' collecting modest commissions for my humble matchmaking services. Very soon, our Chinese partner offered to open a high-end club where 'a respected gentleman could relax after a hard day at the office.' So we did. The business was booming. We were making money hand over fist. I moved out of my parent's apartment into a spacious waterfront place on the Bund facing the Huangpu River. The Bund area got its name from the Urdu 'band,' what means 'embankment.' The Bund was the Wall Street of Asia. It was the center of trade and finance. It was where East met West. It had the most expensive residential arrangements in town.

My parents had never given up on the idea of finding me a proper Russian gentleman. Just to please them, I went along on a few dates resulting in absolute disaster. They couldn't understand that I wasn't that girl, they had brought from Russia. I had been transformed into a worldly, cosmopolitan woman interested in a much bigger world than their confined Russian community. Although the community was prospering. By the mid-1920s, the situation of the Russian émigrés in Shanghai had considerably improved. Many began moving into the French Concession quarter. The Russians had opened dozens of shops, restaurants, and grocery stores on the main road, Avenue Joffre. Soon, the number of the Russian residents had outgrown fourfold the 'native' French population. They started calling it 'The Russian Concession'.

I had dated my own parade of suitors. Some of them were well-known Russians. Maybe, you've heard of Fyodor Shalyapin, the

famous bass opera singer. Yup... I had dated the old man...
He was twice my age, at the time. It didn't last for too long,
anyway. He wasn't that good with his other tool, as he was with
his voice. You know what I mean..."

She rolled her eyes to the ceiling, then looked at me, making
sure I was awake, and continued,

"Then, there was a younger one — a poet, Alexander Vertinsky.
He was in his thirties. He came to the club once and frequented
for some time after. With him, that went on for a bit longer. He
was always coming and going, touring the world. He went to
America, too. I heard he was very popular over there. He sang
sometimes, to the pleasure of my guests. He was some
character... After all, he had married one of my dance-girls and
had a child. Too bad, the idiot later returned to the Soviet Union.
I had lost track of him then. I hope he survived...

Oh..., many dates, many dates... It is hard to remember. But
none of them really lasted, until one day Marco Polo showed up."

She giggled as a school girl, shifted in her deep armchair
under the lampshade, and continued,

"I'm not kidding you. His name was indeed Marco Polo. He was
an Italian merchant ship captain. When he first introduced
himself, I had the same reaction you just had now. We hit it off
from the very first moment we met. Sometimes, he was gone on
his long journeys for a few months. But every time, when he
came back, we had days of paradise. Then one day, he got on his
knee and asked me to marry him! We got married! We did it in a
newly-built Russian church in the French Concession. It had been
done more for my Papa and Mama to make them happy. That
was some wedding, I must tell you. Apparently, I was quite
popular in all foreign communities of Shanghai, and in some
Chinese circles, as well. Marco and I spent our honeymoon in

Thailand. When we came back, we settled in my apartment on the Bund. We were happy together when he returned home from his long trips. I had never considered moving with him back to his home country. Although he kept asking about it.

Then the war broke out. It started out of a small skirmish between the Chinese and the Japanese troops. Oddly enough, it had happened at the 'Marco Polo Bridge,' a large bridge southwest of Beijing, bearing the same name as my husband's. In November of 1937, the Japanese had occupied Shanghai. My Marco was away on one of his long voyages, and that time he couldn't return. The Japanese had closed China. We got stuck worlds apart. He was in Venice, and I was in Shanghai.

The Japanese occupied the entire city, leaving the French Concession relatively independent. They also left alone the International Settlement area, where I and the foreigners lived, mostly the British and the Americans. The rest of the city was destroyed. I had outlived my welcome there. I should've gone away with Marco long time ago. It was too late now. All roads out had been closed, except for just one. It was the most unexpected way out."

She shifted in her chair and looked at me from under her lampshade, making sure I was still listening. Nicolá sprawled in his armchair, spreading his legs far out into the dark room. His eyes were closed lulled into sleep by the monotonous sound of the strange language. It was too much for his first lesson in Russian.

"No ship traffic was going in and out of Shanghai except for regular boats to Tokyo. I had uneasy feelings about things going on in Shanghai. With the war raging throughout China, it could only get worse. Perhaps, it was the same premonition, my Papa had about things in Russia just before the Revolution.

I guess it ran in the family. Just like Papa had done twenty years before, I bought my way out of China and boarded a boat to Tokyo. I heard that merchant ships from Europe had been still coming to Tokyo. Maybe Marco could find a way to pick me up from there. I locked my apartment and left, without telling anyone. I took with me all the money I had saved, tightly packed in a suitcase. When I arrived in Tokyo, I made my way to Yokohama, just south of the city. It was a home to the biggest Chinatown in Japan. With my knowledge of Chinese, I had a better chance of blending into familiar surroundings. It didn't take me too long to make local connections and find a partner to open a dance club there. I had to settle down for a long wait. I didn't know when and how I would get to see Marco again. All my letters came back unanswered.

Another year passed by, and the word about my club got around. It reached someone in Tokyo. I had a visitor, and an offer I couldn't refuse. I left my partner to mind the Yokohama's club and moved to Tokyo. Meanwhile, I heard that the war had broken out in Europe. The Nazis had invaded Poland. Oddly, my beloved China was fighting with Japan, the country that welcomed me in. It was a crazy, crazy world! It had become even crazier when Japan had eventually gotten into the World War.

My business was booming thanks to the thousands of soldiers transiting through Tokyo and looking for fun. By then, I owned a share in a few clubs and in a Geisha house. The life was good. The only dark cloud on my horizon was that I had never heard from Marco, in spite of my many inquiries.

If in Shanghai everything about my business was 'black and white,' in Japan it was much more convoluted. A dance club was indeed a dance club, and nothing more. But, it was a doorway to other services, men were looking for.

Traditional Japanese were not strangers to sexual delights, and men were not constrained to be faithful to their wives. The ideal wife was a modest mother and the home keeper. For sexual enjoyment and even romantic attachment, men didn't go to their wives but to courtesans. Tokyo had designated 'pleasure quarters' outside of which prostitution was illegal. The highest courtesan's class was called Oiran. The Oirans were a combination of actress and prostitute. Geishas who worked within the same pleasure quarters were forbidden to sell sex, not to compete with the Oirans. Geishas carved out a separate niche for themselves, though. They were artists and erudite female companions.

By the time I had arrived on the scene and figured out all the intricacies of that world, geishas were doing everything already. The business was booming again... Until one day, when the two atomic bombs had landed on Hiroshima and Nagasaki. At that very moment, I realized I had to get back to Europe, and fast. The war was over by then.

Once again, I packed my suitcases full of money and boarded a ship bound for Istanbul — the city, where my Papa wanted to take us thirty years ago, fleeing the Russian Revolution. There, with a brief layover, I bought my passage to Genoa. My legs were shaking when I walked down the gangway. I had finally reached my husband's country. I could've been there a dozen years earlier. Well, it was my luck! I had missed the war and had a good life in Tokyo! Most importantly, I was still alive and well."

She stopped for a second as if trying to rewind her life back in her memory,

"I went straight to Marco's house in Venice. When a young woman saw me coming to the door, she started screaming, almost wailing, so all the neighbors came out. Then, she ran and embraced me, still crying, until someone helped to sit her down. The woman was Marco's younger sister. She recognized me from the photographs Marco had brought home — our wedding pictures. We went inside the house and sat down around the table. She didn't say a word, just aimlessly stared out through the window. Her husband came back from work and the kids returned from school. We still kept sitting without saying a word. Finally, she gathered her strength, took me by the hand, and led out to a motor boat. Her husband was waiting for us. We crossed the bay to the other side and walked to a small cemetery. There in the family plot, my Marco was sleeping. He had been killed at the very end of the war. He fought on the side of the Resistance against the Nazis and was mortally wounded in a gunfight in the northern Alps. She pointed to the empty plot next to him, and said, crying, she knew that one day I would find my way home."

It seemed that our hostess kept reliving that moment over and over again. For a while, she stayed quiet. Then she took out a small, pink handkerchief from her long sleeve, and put it carefully against each eye, and continued,

"I have never returned. I decided that I will go back there only once more, to join him. As they say, the rest is history. I had enough money saved to live comfortably for the rest of my life, but I had been too restless just to fade away. So I went back in business. I went back to the only thing I had always known well."

She sat silent for a while,

"Well boys, I thank you for the company tonight. Nowadays, it is very rare when I get a chance to hear the Russian language. It was my pleasure, indeed. Come back soon."

She got up, and turned to me,

"By the way, this one is on me! The rain check…, for tonight!"

*****

I became a once-in-a-while visitor at the establishment. Sometimes, I used the services, the others—just had a cup of tea with the Madam, who customarily kept talking in her native tongue all the time. There was not much room left for me to speak Russian. Once I asked her if by any chance her last name was *Golubov*. I could see her face turning pale, even through a heavy makeup. I thought that she was having a heart attack, and summoned the butler. It looked that the man was trained and used to different kinds of emergencies possible in the establishment of that kind. He came prepared with a defibrillator machine, ice packs, syringes and medicines of undetermined nature. Luckily, we didn't need any. The Madam came to quickly, gained her usual color, and said, but quietly,

"For over forty years, I didn't hear anyone say my last name. I have been using my late husband's surname — Polo."

"I may have a surprise for you, madam!" I said. "But you have to promise me not to scare us with going pale like that. Promise?"

*****

9. The Full Circle

I ended up staying in Italy for three more years. When my first year was finished, Joseph Wieber personally flew to Milan and asked me to stay for another year on behalf of *"Wieber Scientific Products"*. How could I refuse? The only condition, I asked for, was to hire another person. Frank wouldn't have to run from Munich to help me every time I drowned in work. With my expanded staff, I freed more time for my other endeavor with Mr. Alfonsi. When I returned from London, I told Evgeny Koblukov that as much as I appreciated his offer, it wasn't for me. I kept running into him in the office occasionally but had not spoken to him. It appeared that he lost any interest, too, and didn't bother me. I suspected that Mr. Alfonsi had interfered on my behalf. He was more important to the KGB than I was. It suited me just fine. Meanwhile, I hired two more people to handle the ever-growing amount of work for Mr. Alfonsi's new business with Russia.

Nicolá had become a new liaison between his father and Evgeny Koblukov. Although Nicolá had to spend more time in the office than he had ever spent before, he had made sure he always had time for his other passion. Nicolá liked women. It by itself wasn't anything unusual, but in Nicolá's case, it went far beyond ordinary. He did not discriminate. He liked them all — white, black, yellow — as long as they were attractive and willing to surrender to his charms. Lately, he took a liking to exotic women, the way he put it himself. At that time, it was difficult to find exotic women in Italy. On the other hand, our Russian madam-friend could easily accommodate his desires. Every time, he returned from a visit to her establishment, for the entire morning, he kept talking about an Asian girl he was with the night before. He couldn't wait till his dad would open the Moscow office. He was saving his true passion for the Russian blonds he hoped to charm there.

One night, I was about to turn off the lights and get out of the office when Nicolá appeared in my door. He was heavy breathing as if he just finished running a hundred-meter dash.

"You must come with me at once. I have a surprise for you…"

I was used to his surprises and followed him to his car. We drove to a small restaurant, we both liked and frequented. The place had a dozen tables and was known for a family-style northern Italian cooking. It was still early in the evening when we walked in. The restaurant was empty, except for an oval table set by the window. Two older women sat there with their backs turned towards us. A young woman was sitting with them, facing us. It was Josie. It had been over a year since that spring in London when I saw her last time. Professor Golubov and the Madam sat quietly, holding hands.

"We have not seen each other for forty years," Professor Golubov almost whispered. "I still see her apartment in Shanghai on that day when I had found it empty. My dear sister had vanished in the thin air. And now, here we are together again, thanks to you, boys."

She got up and kissed me on the cheek as if I was the only one who deserved all the credit. The Madam was holding a pink handkerchief against her eyes.

"I am trying to help with a visa to bring Professor Golubov's sister to the States for a visit," Josie interrupted an awkward silence. "We are running into some resistance because…," she paused, "… because of the nature of the business, Professor Golubov's sister is involved. I think I found a loophole in the law...," Josie smiled. "They will be together in the States soon."

*****

When my second year came to an end, I agreed to stay for a few more months to help a new guy who arrived from the States to replace me. He happened to speak Italian that he learned from his grandparents growing up in Brooklyn. It was an easy transition for him. I remained in Milan even after the fellow took over my job. At that time, it was Mr. Alfonsi who begged me to stay.

The Italians had started modernizing an old car factory in a godforsaken village some five hundred miles east of Moscow. *"Fiat"* had built the factory almost twenty years ago. By the time Mr. Alfonsi got involved, that remote village had been transformed into a town. They had named it *Tolyatti*, after the Italian Communist Party leader *Palmiro Togliatti*. The car that the factory produced had been named *"Lada,"* after the wife of famous ancient Russian Prince Igor. The Soviet leaders envisioned it as a "people's car," just like *"Citroën" was* in France or *"VW Beetle"* in Germany. *"Lada"* was some crap of a car, and with a capital C! In spite of that, cops and cabbies quickly adopted it. Private citizens were allowed to buy it freely, too, as long as they had the money. A very tiny sliver of the population of three hundred million people could afford it. The ones who could, had to deal with the ever-growing headache of the scarcity of gas, car parts and everything else a car required. There was a popular saying going around, loosely translated,

"If you want a girlfriend, buy yourself a 'Lada' instead. It will always be on top of you..."

Mr. Alfonsi hired a few more people who worked on commissions translating mountains of technical documentation. Once their handy-work reached Russia, it became a disaster. The Russian engineers couldn't understand large chunks of their translations. People, who Mr. Alfonsi had hired, had no technical education. They had translated complicated documents into some street gibberish that had no sense. Once again, I had to interview a new bunch of people Mr. Alfonsi was desperately searching throughout Europe to hire. I went through three dozen of applicants and had found two. We kept searching and hired two more. With the six full-time more-or-less technical people and two secretaries, the new office was abuzz around the clock. Someone had to manage that chaos. It took me another year to make that office run smoothly, when all of a sudden, all the work had stopped. The Italians had finished their project, got paid (whatever they managed to collect from the Russians), and gone back home. My job was done. I was done with Europe, too.

Finally, I was ready to return to the USA. I went around to bid farewell to all people I had crossed my path with. Many of my colleagues and customers were upset, hearing I was to abandon them soon. Yet, my Italian friends were sincerely happy for me as if they were going home to America themselves.

Nicolá threw a big party. Of course, after the party, I wanted to pay a visit to our madam-friend from Shanghai.

"My dear friend, it is not going to happen!" sad Nicolá and rolled his eyes to the sky.

"What happened?" I couldn't help but exclaim. "What happened to her? Did she pass away?"

I was really scared. For the first time in my adult life, I realized that sooner or later we were going to lose people we were attached to. Although I wouldn't call the Madam my friend, I grew to like her. I liked her quiet manners and her stories. They put me to sleep sometimes, but they stuck in my memory.

"Well," Nicolá started after pausing long enough to savor the moment, then continued,

"We would need to take a ride to Venice. Our Madam had gotten an offer to sell her business. She did, and with the handsome proceeds, she bought a large, old palazzo on the island of Burano. It is one of the many islands in the Venice Lagoon surrounding the city. The building belonged to one of many dilapidated estates a noble family couldn't support any longer. She put a ton of money in restoring it to its previous splendor. The place is a stone-throw away from the cemetery where her husband is buried. I heard that she persuaded his sister's family to move in with her."

Nicolá was right, the Madam must have spent a small fortune to make the palazzo inhabitable. It was a three-story eighteen- century building, once belonging to a French count. The twenty-feet high ceilings were adorned with paintings of voluptuous naked women and as voluptuous oversized angels. The walls were covered with tapestries depicting hunting scenes from unidentified European royalty.
The quality of the tapestry was just as high as I had seen in the Vatican museums.

The Madam was excited about her new life. She looked refreshed and energetic while showing us her new digs.

While walking around, she revealed that the American authorities kept denying her visa application, citing her occupation, until Josie helped her to prove that the Madam intended to invest in the US a significant amount of money. Apparently, the US government couldn't care less what business, the Madam had intended to open, as long as she brought one million dollars and hired people. Finally, the Madam could enter the United States. She flew to visit her sister Professor Golubov in Connecticut.

They had spent the entire summer together with Nana Rachel at her estate on the pond. A few times, they had visited New York city where they stayed for a while. The Madam discovered that there was indeed a need to establish her business in the Big Apple. After all, she was successful in Shanghai, Tokyo, and Milan. There was a problem, though. She realized that she didn't have her energy to do it, she wasn't young anymore. Just before leaving America, the Madam offered to finance the entire enterprise under two conditions. Her sister Professor Golubov and Nana Rachel will own it. The name of the establishment should be "The Shanghai Club."

The Madam was perhaps the only one in the entire country who was genuinely disappointed by my departure from Italy. *"Those barbarians in the New World! What do they know from culture? Tell me? What do they know? Young man, you belong here in Europe! You belong here in Italy!"* I couldn't argue with the Madam. She was kind to me. She and her girls were very, very kind.

*****

Soon after, we went to visit our friend Velia. She got married recently to a count of some small-fiefdom fame. Against any conventional wisdom, Italy did not exist as a country until just a hundred years ago. It was a loose union of constantly quarreling small kingdoms and counties. Of course, that particular fiefdom Velia married into didn't exist any longer, but the royal lineage had been kept in the minds of its ancestors. Velia lived in a castle in a Piedmont countryside. However small that castle was, it was surrounded by tall walls and a moat with a real tiny drawbridge, you could only see in medieval paintings or in the movies.

Velia came out to greet us to the other side of a narrow moat. She looked stunning, dressed in beige breeches tucked into high riding boots. On top, she had a see-through crème blouse, leaving nothing to the imagination. Her breasts perked under the blouse, exposing large, dark-brown nipples.

"That piece of sh*t, the husband of mine, left this thing up." She pointed to the bridge. "He does it all the time, just to play with his remote. I'd rather him play with something else. He can't get his own thing up..."

Velia produced this strange monologue while cranking the bridge gears down. We walked across and took turns hugging her. It was an unusually prolonged hug, one wouldn't expect from a married woman. Velia led the way inside a courtyard surrounded by the thick walls. The castle looked in disrepair. As if reading my mind, Velia said,

"We live in this part. I've been here for over a year, but never ventured to the other side. It would cost a fortune to fix this sh*thole. My husband's family is broke. The only thing they still hold onto is their family name and the title. I am *la Contessa* now, in case you two commoners forget. I suspect they married me to use my money to fix this dump."

We entered the castle and went up a spiral stone stairway to the second-floor balcony overlooking the back. As far as the eye could see, the green Piedmont hills stretched to the horizon.

"See, all these vineyards," she pointed out. "These are all owned by my family, but this ruin is his. Now that I got my title, I am thinking to divorce him. I am not a farm girl." She stopped, and quickly added, "Maybe, I am… Let me show you something, boys."

We walked down and exited to the back of the castle. Velia headed to a small greenhouse and opened its door.

"It is here, where I do my farming…"

The place had a few orderly rows of healthy cannabis bushes. A table sat along the wall. It had a few wooden boxes filled with rolled joints.

"Help yourselves! Don't be shy, boys,"

"Velia, we hoped you could introduce us to your husband," I started cautiously. The things were moving too fast.

"Husband? What husband?" Velia pretended. "He went to visit his Mama in Rome, to cry on her lap about me leaving him. *Bastardo!*"

She grabbed a small box from the shelf above the table,

"These are my reserve stash, the best quality! Go for it, gents!"

We settled on a bluestone porch overlooking the backyard, what in essence, was Velia's family vineyard taking up the entire hill. The evening started to blanket the valley below.

"My family has been growing grapes here since…, I think, forever. The best wines come from this soil. There is no price to pay for this land. I am priceless! Once I get rid of my Bastardo husband, I will be a priceless countess, boys!"

Velia got up and ran inside. She brought out glasses and a bottle of red wine. Then, she ran down the hill and returned holding in her hand a cluster of grapes.

"Boys, this is *Nebbiolo*, a local grape. We make two wines out of it." She pointed to the bottle on the table, "this *'Barbaresco'*, and the other one is *'Barolo.'* They are made from the same grape, and less than ten miles apart, but so different."

Velia was excited talking about her wines. Her cheeks got pink and the eyes were sparkling. I remembered that Nicolá once mentioned that all he knew about wines he had learned from her. Again, Velia disappeared for a few minutes, and returned holding a bottle of *"Barolo"*.

"One can always tell the difference between those two. We have a local river called Tanaro. It cuts Piedmont across. The same grape grows a bit faster on the south bank and ripens quicker, giving *'Barbaresco'* its light-red. The grape grown on the north bank takes a tad longer to ripen. That is enough to make out of it dark-red and heavier *'Barolo'*. With that, I will conclude your wine lesson for tonight, boys."

We sat outside till the first stars started popping up in the dark-blue sky. By that time, we were pretty wasted and asked if we could crash in her castle, sparing us drive back to Milan.

"I didn't drag you boys all the way up here, to just let you go. We are having a party, the farewell party for you. Didn't you come to say goodbye? Oh, by the way, how is your girlfriend Josie doing in London? Did I get her name right?"

"We haven't seen each other for almost four years, since that Christmas in Siena."

"Oh... I am so sorry," Velia seemed genuinely upset for me. "Okay, then that makes it much easier," Velia jumped up. "I suggest I show you the castle's main bedroom. I hope you boys didn't forget my rules: No double-dipping, and I always require a fresh rubber. Let's go party!"

*****

I didn't realize that I had accumulated so much stuff in four years until I started to pack. I had arrived in Italy with one suitcase. Now I needed four. Certainly, the exchange rate helped me. It was like buying everything at half-price.
I suppose that all these good Italian clothes and leather shoes could last me for another thirty years. I just had to watch my waistline.

I flew home. What a sweet word – "home." As much as I was welcomed by America and its people, I still didn't have the home to come back to. Josie's family tried hard to make me feel home. Nana Rachel went out of her way too. My little cottage on the pond had been my home, the only one I knew since I left Russia almost nine years ago. And now, I was on the way back, just to find that there was no cottage on the pond anymore. Nana Rachel sold the estate and moved to New York City. It happened suddenly. No one expected it. No one even knew where she was in the city. I tried to look for her friend Professor Golubov. No one at the UConn knew what happened to her after she abruptly retired. It all happened fast.

I arrived back in the office to find that my company had created a new department of international sales and offered me a position. I had a week to think it over while living at the Inn on the company's dime. I asked for the same room, I had stayed before. When I unlocked the door, I saw Josie sleeping naked on my bed. I flipped the light switch, and she was gone. Then the phone rang. *"Who could possibly know that I was back in the States sitting in a hotel room in the middle of the Connecticut farmlands?"*

"Darling, welcome home," I heard a voice of Professor Golubov.

She was the last person, I expected to find on the other end. I sat silent, not able to say a word.

"Are you still there, darling? It must be a bad connection. Let me redial at once. Stay where you are."

She was about to hang up when I finally could squeeze a greeting of a surprise out of my mouth.

"Why don't you, darling, take a morning train to New York. I hope you didn't forget your way back, and the old stomping ground."

I didn't know what to say. I had all the time in the world for a week. I saved some money. Why not take a little time off. I deserved it. After all, I had some vacation time left, too.

"Are you still there, darling... This bad connection..."

"I'll be there tomorrow."

She gave me the address. After a small talk, we hung up. I remembered Josie telling me that sometimes, Nana Rachel shared her desire to move to the big city. She dreamed about "the Great White Way" of Broadway, the Central Park, the museums, and galleries... Then I also remembered that the Madam mentioned something about her investing in America.

I took Metro-North train to the Grand Central Station and walked up Park Avenue for thirty blocks to East 76th street and turned west to the Central Park. I found a brownstone in the middle of the block between Madison and the Fifth Avenue. A few steps up brought me to a small landing where I found myself in front of the door with an elaborately engraved brass plate *"The Shanghai Club."*

I pushed a matching brass doorbell. It seemed they expected me. The door opened even before I managed to push on the bell for the second time. A man dressed in a crisp tuxedo, wearing white gloves, appeared in the door. He bowed his head and waved his hand to come in. Something seemed familiar in his gesture. I followed inside of a small lobby. My attention was attracted by the framed paintings on the walls depicting images of old St. Petersburg before the Russian Revolution of 1917. I probably stood there for a while before noticing that the man in the tuxedo was watching me. He waited till I switched my eyes from the paintings onto him and quietly said,

"Please, go on in this room. They are waiting for you."

I opened the door and found a large space, rather looking as a ballroom. Tall windows draped in heavy, velvet dark-red curtains brought back the memories of Milan. Expensive French couches and armchairs were casually scattered around the room. Suddenly, the door on the other end opened, and Professor Golubov made her entrance. She seemed younger, taller and very stylish. I wouldn't recognize her on the street. *What happened to the proper professor I remembered...*

Ms. Golubov had a short hairdo. Her hair was dyed in dark-brown. She probably had a face-lift done, and... the teeth. She was dressed in a formal two-piece, light-beige suit, complemented by high hills in matching color. Small, golden earrings and a pearl necklace completed the ensemble. *What the hell had happened to our professor...?*

"Please, come in, don't be a stranger, darling."

Even her voice took on some resemblance of a British accent... She kissed me lightly on the cheek and led to two armchairs separated by an elaborate coffee table. The man in the tuxedo entered pushing a cart with the Samovar, china, and bite-size sandwiches. We talked about the benefits of living in the city. Looking around, I noticed a photograph of a child in an expensive silver frame standing on a coffee table by the wall across. The picture seemed out of place in that formal room. It looked like one of those pictures, department stores use to sell the frames. I could see it in a family den or a bedroom. A girl in the picture had a full-head of dark curls. Her big, dark eyes reminded me of a pair of ripe grapes.

Every time, I tried to look away, the child's eyes kept following me. I felt that the child was present in the room. Ms. Golubov noticed that I kept glancing at the picture but didn't say anything. A few more minutes went by. Finally, she shifted in her chair and said,

"Why don't you take a look at it."

I got up and took the frame. It was a boy, not a girl as I thought. A strangely familiar face was looking at me from the picture. Ten years ago, when I was leaving the Soviet Union, the authorities allowed to take out a few photographs. My mother packed some family photos and a few pictures of me taken at different ages. One particular photograph had been taken when I was three years old.

Now, standing in the middle of New York City and holding that frame in my hands, I realized that the child in the picture had a close resemblance to myself at that very age. The picture was taken on the bank of the River Thames, with the London Tower bridge behind him.

"This is David, our grandson," Ms. Golubov said proudly.

"Our grandson?" I thought. *"How strange...,"* but didn't say anything. Meanwhile, she continued,

"He is now staying with Josie's parents in Connecticut until she settles in Geneva with her new assignment."

She took the picture out of my hands,

"It is a strange world. I remember you told us about your Grandfather, who once lived in New York..."

Indeed, my father's father came to America in the early 1900s. He lived here for a while and went back to Belarussia to get married to my future grandmother Lia. He never returned to America. The Russian Communist revolution had happened. Twenty-five years later, they had found their death from the Nazis who invaded their homeland. My Grandfather's name was David. I saw Ms. Golubov was carefully watching me. Then she suddenly said, putting back on the British accent,

"I suppose we don't need any DNA proof here... Josie had decided to have this child. She was too proud to let you know after you had ended your relation with her so abruptly. She never married. Perhaps, if you still care, you should..." Ms. Golubov stopped in the middle of the sentence.

She carefully placed the frame with the child back and walked to her armchair. We sat quietly for a long time, as if afraid to disturb the precious moment.

"Professor Golubov," I broke the silence first. "What a transformation. This city certainly has a positive effect on you. How long do you plan to visit here? The school is about to start. Nice digs, too. Thank you for thinking of me. I could use a few days to unwind in the big city..."

I didn't get to finish and froze with my mouth half-open. Nana Rachel entered the room. She was as elegant as her friend. She too seemed taller and younger. Nana Rachel came to me, and let me kiss her. Then she softly said,

"Well, my young friend, it is not what you could even imagine...," Nana Rachel paused.

She walked to Professor Golubov, took her hand in hers, and almost whispered,

"I would like to introduce to you Ms. Golubov, the Madam and the owner of the newest club in New York, *"The Shanghai Club."*

The Madam Golubov looked at Nana Rachel, giggled and chimed in,

"Miss Rachel is my partner in the Club. She manages our business affairs."

###

Copyright Acknowledgment

<u>Cover Design by URI NORWICH</u>

Cover Photographic Work by **Dennis Mayk**, used pursuant to "Creative Commons Zero" Public Domain License agreement with www.unsplash.com©

<u>Back Cover Design by URI NORWICH</u>

Photographic Work used pursuant to "Creative Commons CC0" Public Domain License Agreement of the authors with www.pixabay.com ©

Notebook-Pen, by Cimedia. Public Domain License

Publisher's logo is the property of **"highwood publishing new york©"**

******

This Book is available as **e-Book** format

ISBN-13: 978-1370495788

www.amazon.com

www.smashwords.com

for devices offered by

- **Kindle® (Amazon)**
- **Apple®**
- **Android® based**
- **Barnes and Noble®**
- **Sony®, and others**

All inquiries address to **highwoodpublishingny@gmail.com**

Thank you for reading my book.

Uri Norwich

Author can be contacted at **urinorwich@gmail.com**

Read Interview with the Author at

www.smashwords.com/interview/urinorwich

Also By Uri Norwich
"Russian Jews Don't Cry"© 2013-2016
"If I Was Real... "©2013-2016
"The American Deluge"©2014

Made in the USA
Las Vegas, NV
28 September 2021